POKER FACE

LINDSEY POWELL

Content copyright © Lindsey Powell 2021
Cover design by Lindsey Powell & Wicked Dreams Publishing 2021

All rights reserved. No part of this book may be reproduced or utilised in any form, or by any electronic or mechanical means, without the prior written permission of the author.

The characters and events portrayed in this book are fictional. Any similarities to other fictional workings, or real persons (living or dead), names, places, and companies is purely coincidental and not intended by the author.

The right of Lindsey Powell to be identified as the author of this work has been asserted by her in accordance with the Copyright, Designs and Patents act 1988.

A CIP record of this book is available from the British Library.

Except for the original material written by the author, all mention of films, television shows and songs, song titles, and lyrics mentioned in the novel, Poker Face, are the property of the songwriters and copyright holders.

BOOKS BY LINDSEY POWELL

The Perfect Series
Perfect Stranger

Perfect Memories

Perfect Disaster

Perfect Beginnings

The Complete Perfect Series

Part of Me Series
Part of Me

Part of You

Part of Us

The Control Duet
Losing Control

Taking Control

Stand-alone
Take Me

Fixation

Checkmate

A Valentine Christmas

CHAPTER ONE

SITTING ON THE DESK, I lean back, my hands going behind me, my fingers wrapping around the edging to hold me up as I uncross my legs and widen them, leaving nothing to the imagination. I lick my lips as I watch the lust ignite in his eyes. He didn't expect me to be bare beneath my skirt. He didn't expect me to rock in here and expose myself to him.

But I did.

And here I am.

Exposed, turned on, and desperately hoping that he doesn't push me away.

I'm not a needy bitch, but I go after what I want, and what I want is him.

Jesse Marks.

The most deliciously handsome man that I have ever seen.

Every girl wants him.

Every woman wants him.

But they don't get to have him, because he's mine and I'll make damn sure of it.

I don't love him, but I don't think it would be hard to fall for his natural charm. I don't even think he realises just how fucking sexy he is, and that makes him even sexier.

His light-green eyes are still on my pussy, his jaw clenched, his hands balled into fists.

"What's the matter, sir? Don't you like what you see?" I say seductively. I may only be nineteen, but I know my own mind. Nobody plays me, I play them. Young and stupid they may call me, but you only live once. And I've always lived on the edge with my parents being well-known in the underworld, I've always been driving in the fast lane. I don't have time for weakness, I don't have the patience for people to dream of what they want and then do fuck all about it.

"Natalie, what are you doing?" he says, his voice washing over me, his tone tantalising me.

"Don't play dumb with me, sir, I think it's very clear what I'm doing," I reply, hitching my skirt up a little more by moving one of my legs and placing my foot on the arm of his office chair, my knee bent slightly, my pussy anticipating the moment that he gives in.

"You shouldn't be here," he says, his eyes holding mine, the look he's giving me doing nothing to back up his words.

"And why's that?" I say. I think it's sweet he's trying to dodge what is going to happen here, but he'd be stupid to believe that I was just going to walk away. I never walk away.

"For one, it's inappropriate. Two, it's unethical. Three, your father would kill me if he ever found out," he says, and I feel my eyes light up at his words because he never said he didn't want me, he just gave me bullshit reasons as to why we shouldn't do this.

"So, you're scared of my father?" I say, feeling slightly amused.

"I'm not scared, but I think most people would feel a little nervous around your father," he scoffs.

I smirk. "You ever met my mother?"

"Once."

"Well, let me tell you something, sir"—I move my other leg to the other arm of his chair and widen them a little more—"Never underestimate how powerful the female is. You may think that we don't have our shit all figured out, but we absolutely do. I know what I want, I know what I need, and I know that I don't give a fuck what anyone thinks."

"I don't underestimate you, Natalie, far from it." The way my name rolls off his tongue has goosebumps trailing over my skin. I've always loved the way he says my name. His deep, gravelly voice captivates me.

"Good, so then you will know that I'm not moving from this desk until your mouth is on me... Until your dick is inside of me... Until I am screaming your name because no other words exist. We've been dancing around each other for the last three months, and I'm tired of dancing. I want you to fuck me, *sir*."

"Fuck," he breathes out, the air whooshing from his lungs as I see him wrestling with his emotions.

"You can be the good guy or the bad but let me tell you this... Nice guys always finish last," I say as I move my hand from the desk and run my fingers up the inside of my thigh, pushing my skirt up.

I see his nostrils flare as I let my finger brush against my pussy, a shudder going through me.

"Do you want me, sir? Do you want to feel how good your cock is inside of me? Do you want to feel my lips against yours? Do you want to feel that rush that only I can give you?" I tease him, knowing that he's never done anything like this, and knowing that he wants me just as much as I want him.

"Anyone could walk in here," he says, and I know that I am winning, grinding him down.

"So?"

"So?" he says, his eyebrows raising.

"Don't you like a little danger?" I say as I move my finger to my opening and push in slowly, dropping my head back and closing my eyes.

"Jesus Christ," I hear him say, and then I feel his hand on my wrist, the one that is currently pushing my finger into my pussy. I open my eyes and lift my head back up, locking my silver-coloured eyes with his.

"Fuck me, Jesse," I say, my voice quiet but showing just how much I want him. "Make me yours."

"God forgive me," he whispers before crashing his mouth onto mine.

My hands are in his hair, pulling his silky brunette locks that are only just long enough to run my fingers through. One of his hands is pressed flat at the bottom of my spine, holding me steady, whilst his other is gripping my hip bone, his fingers biting into my skin. His tongue forcefully massages mine, and I moan into his mouth. We've only just kissed but already I know that this is going to be the most mind-blowing fuck of my short life. I've only ever been with boys before, and by boys, I mean ones that are so fucking scared after meeting my father that they run a mile. I'm sick of boys and tired of them having no fucking backbone.

Now, I'm with a man who knows what he wants, even if he wrestles with his heart and mind to get there.

I break from his lips, my hands falling from his hair and dropping to his trousers. He watches me as I unzip him and pull out his already-erect cock from his pants, quickly whipping out the condom that I had hidden in my bra and ripping the packet open with my teeth before sheathing him completely.

"Once we do this, there is no going back," he says. "The line has already been crossed, Natalie, but just know that if we get found out, I will fight to be with you, I won't give up, and you will be mine, always."

And fuck if those words aren't the best words that I have ever heard.

In answer to his question, I slide myself forwards on his desk and place his cock at my opening.

"I like a man that fights," I purr before I push forwards, his cock going deep inside of me.

His eyes ignite and the man I knew is gone as an animal takes over.

He pulls back and then pounds into me, over and over again. He bites my earlobe, licks my neck, kisses my already-swollen lips.

I wrap my legs around his waist, locking them together as he moves me off of the desk and turns us around, my back hitting the wall as he takes us to the next fucking level. I have only ever been with one other guy, and he had been my boyfriend for a year. A whole year where I wasted my time with a no-hoper who just wanted 'in' with my father. And a whole year where I was subjected to timid fucking that left me having to finish myself off.

I always knew that Jesse would know what he was doing, but I had not prepared myself for the fucking fireworks that are currently exploding inside of me.

I moan out loud as my release builds.

He growls as I tighten my walls around him.

And then I say the words that push him over the edge, taking me with him. "Fuck me harder, Professor, make me come."

And he does.

He makes me come, hard.

My eyes go blurry, my mind becomes hazy, and my pleasure overtakes me.

Jesse crashes his lips back to mine, swallowing both of our

moans as his punishing strokes start to relent as he brings us back to reality. His kisses turn softer, his hands caress gentler, and my heart fucking flutters at the difference.

Professor Jesse Marks.

My teacher.

My mentor.

Someone who is placed in a position of trust.

But sometimes trust is meant to be broken.

My name is Natalie Valentine, and this is my story.

CHAPTER TWO

"**HOW WAS YOUR DAY,** angel?" my dad asks me as I walk into the kitchen to see him sat at the kitchen island, the newspaper spread out in front of him, a cup of coffee beside it, steam rising into the air. My dad is the baddest man I know, but around me, he's like putty in my hands. There isn't anything he wouldn't do for me, or my mum, and it doesn't matter how old I am, I'll always be his baby girl, which he likes to remind me of every now and again.

"It was good thanks, Dad," I say as a smile forms on my lips. It was more than good, but I am not about to tell my dad that my professor just fucked the living daylights out of me.

"Did you get all of your work finished?" he asks. I messaged him to say I would be late home because I had work to do... the "work" being Jesse Marks.

"Yup," I almost sing as I grab a cold can of coke from the fridge. As I close the fridge door, my mum comes into view.

"Hi, sweetie," she says as she comes over, gives me a hug and places a kiss on my cheek.

"Hi, Mum," I reply with a smile. My mum is the most beautiful woman that I have ever seen. Long blond hair, stormy grey eyes, and a killer body even at the age of fifty-two. She doesn't look fifty-two, and my dad doesn't look fifty-five. They've both looked after themselves over the years, and it shows. Most of my friends can't believe that these people are my parents. It always makes me roll my eyes when they make comments about it, because to me, Joey and Paige are just Mum and Dad.

"How was school?" she asks.

"Uni, Mum," I correct her.

She rolls her eyes at me. "Same thing," she says with a flippant wave of her hand. It's not the same thing at all, and when she says school it makes me feel like I am about five fucking years old, which I hate. "Hey, baby," she says to my dad as she walks over to him and kisses him on the cheek. The fucking smile that spreads across my dad's face compares to nothing. He always looks like this when my mum walks into a room; completely in awe of her. She's his queen, and always has been from what they've told me.

She turns back to me, her hands resting on my dad's shoulders. "Steak okay for dinner?"

"Sounds good," I say with a nod of my head. "Want any help?" I offer.

"No, it's okay, your dad can help me," she says, to which my dad lets out a muffled groan. "Problem?" my mum says as my dad tips his head back to look at her.

"No problem," he says. "Can a man finish his coffee first?"

"Can a man not drink his coffee at the same time?" she retorts, one eyebrow raised.

"Happy wife, happy life, right?" he says with a chuckle.

"You know it, Valentine," my mum says before disappearing into the big-ass larder to grab whatever she needs for dinner.

My dad shakes his head as he gets up from his chair. "You

know, I'd only ever take orders like that from your mother," he says.

"I know, Dad." I smile, and he disappears into the larder after my mum. You would think that it would make me feel icky seeing my mum and dad openly sharing affection for one another, but it doesn't because they never cross the line in front of me. Their banter amuses me, and their love is something that I want for myself one day.

They both taught me to never settle for less than I deserve, and it's taken me a few years to really let that sink in. And now I get it. I get it because although going after Jesse is wrong, I couldn't fucking help myself. He may be older than me, he may be my professor, and it may be all shades of wrong, but we're both adults, we're both consenting, and we both know what we're getting ourselves into.

The thing is, he could be 'the one.'

He could be my happy ever after.

He could be the one that challenges me, just like my dad challenges my mum. I don't want a guy that's going to fawn all over me, and I don't want a guy that's going to ignore me because it's the cool thing to do. I want a guy that worships me, but also makes me work. Because I can tell you one thing, I may not quite be twenty years old yet, but I will make him work, and it's going to take one strong motherfucker to put up with me.

CHAPTER THREE

"DON'T FORGET YOUR ASSIGNMENTS are due in tomorrow," Jesse shouts to the class as students make their way out of the room.

I take my time putting my things away, seeing no reason to rush like the rest of them, and if I happen to still be in here when they've all gone, then at least I might be able to speak to Jesse about yesterday. So far, I haven't been able to catch him alone, and I'm almost desperate to see where his head is at. I may come across as a confident woman, and I am to a certain extent, but fuck if I'm not slightly doubting everything I thought I was sure of yesterday.

"You coming to the lunch hall?" I hear Sophia ask from beside me.

"No thanks, I've got some reading to do in the library," I tell her.

"In your lunch hour?" she questions.

"Yeah." I continue to pack my things into my bag, avoiding looking at her.

"Since when do you read in your lunch hour?"

"Since today."

"Uh huh," she says, and I can feel her suspicious eyes on me. Sophia and I have been friends for the last year and a half, since we both started Uni, and both ended up on the same course studying criminal law. Yeah, I know, me, studying criminal law when my parents are notorious in the underworld, and yesterday I had sex with my professor. Ironic, huh?

I look to Sophia, who still hasn't taken her brown-coloured eyes off of me. "What is the matter with me studying at lunch?" I say with a shrug of my shoulders.

"It's just not something you have ever done in the last year and a half," she states.

Bugger. She's going to catch on if I don't think on my feet, and quick.

"Look, I've been struggling with the assignment regarding the Goldman case," I tell her. "I need to try and read it through again and get my head around it." The Goldman case is one that could portray some of the shit I'm sure my parents have done in their time. The head of a mafia family, Goldman dealt in drugs, had runners from here to America, his name was well-known around the world, until one of his runners turned rogue, got jealous, wanted more time in the spotlight and set Goldman up to fail. And fail he did, falling prey to the runner's traps, thinking he was giving intel to one of his most trusted, only for his runner to be working with the police to bring him down. Add into that that Goldman tortured the runner, the police finding him at the last minute, with the runner hanging onto his life by a thread. The assignment is about how the runner laid the traps and manipulated a man that once ruled high and mighty. We have to research where it all went wrong, and give our interpretation of how the runner turned, the why's, the where's and the what if's before detailing what we would have done as the prosecutors of such a high-profile case. I'm not struggling with it at all, but

I need to throw Sophia off of whatever scent she's picking up from me.

"Oh, well, you want me to bring some lunch to you?" she offers, backing off a little bit.

"No, I'm good, got a steak sandwich left over from dinner last night," I tell her.

"Oh, man, steak?"

"Yup."

"Your mum is the fucking best," Sophia says.

"I know." I am under no illusions that my mum is a fucking saint when it comes to me, I don't fancy any other fuckers' chances mind. Sophia doesn't really know what my parents do, and I have no intention of informing her. All she knows is that we live in a big-ass house and my parents wear fancy suits to an office job. Technically not lying, seeing as they do wear suits and they work in the office of their club, Club Valentine. They may not run the game anymore, but they sure as shit don't let anyone cross them. Not that I've ever been privy to see what they do, but I've heard enough to know that they are still feared in the world we live in. My Aunt Meghan and Uncle Miles have told me a few stories in the last couple of years, so I am under no illusion that if you fuck with my parents, they go after you twice as hard.

"Okay, well, I'll see you in next period," Sophia says before flouncing off, her curly red hair swaying as she goes.

Finally, it's just me and Jesse.

And he's looking at me like I'm a goddamn cream cake.

Excellent.

I walk down the steps, slowly, savouring how his eyes devour me with every movement. I come to a stop on the other side of his desk and have to physically remind myself to fucking breathe.

He stands there, his hands in his pockets, his dark chocolate-coloured hair slightly swept to one side, his green eyes alight with desire, his broad shoulders begging me to rip his goddamn shirt from him.

Oof.

I lick my lips, wishing that we could just lock ourselves away from the world for a little while.

"Sir, I need some help with my assignment," I say, breaking the silence that surrounds us.

"And what help might that be?" he says, one eyebrow raised.

"I just need a little help with which direction I should go... Should I let go and watch as what I really want to happen moves further away from me? Or should I do what my heart desires and fight tooth and nail for something that I know could have the best outcome, even if things will be tricky along the way?" I say, the double meaning behind my words obvious.

Jesse's eyes sweep around the room and to the door, which is open.

"This isn't really the place to talk about it," he says quietly.

"No? Then where is?" I say, tilting my head to the side.

"My office."

"When?"

"Now."

"Okay. Lead the way," I say as I gesture for him to lead me to his domain.

He smirks, picking up his folder off of the desk and I follow as he leads me from the room, down the corridor and into his office which has frosted windows, making it an added bonus that no one can see exactly what we're up to in here.

He shuts the door and I feel a shiver run through me as he turns to face me.

Before either of us can speak, we're making our way towards each other, the items we were carrying now discarded to the floor, and then our lips are meeting, his hands are round my waist and mine are linked around his neck. It's like we've been apart for days rather than hours. It's like we've been lovers for years rather than just two people who decided to take their relationship to the next level... not even twenty-four hours ago.

"You haven't changed your mind then?" he whispers between kisses.

"No," I reply breathlessly as he trails his lips down my neck.

"This is insane," he says as he keeps moving lower until he's pulling my top and bra down and covering my nipple with his mouth. A few flicks of his tongue and I'm desperate for him to claim me all over again.

I throw my head back as his teeth graze my nipple and I move my hand down and grab his dick through his trousers.

"It's not insane," I say as I unzip him and push my hand into his boxers.

He moves me backwards until I'm against the wall, his hands going either side of my head, his eyes connecting with mine.

"It is, Natalie, and you know it," he says before a moan escapes as I wrap my fingers around him and pump up and down.

"Why? Because I'm a student?"

"Yes," he says.

"But even if we had met in a bar, I'd still be a student."

"You wouldn't be *my* student."

"If that's your argument then you fucking lose, Professor," I say as I pump my hand faster.

"Then there's the age difference," he says through gritted teeth as he struggles to contain his release.

I smirk. "Age is just a number."

"I would be struck off," he counters.

"You knew that before you put your dick in me yesterday."

"Your parents would probably kill me," he continues.

"True, but then they love me and want me to be happy, so it's either kill you and hurt me or let you live and watch me be happy. No contest really." Shit would not go down this smoothly, I know that, but I have his dick in my hand and I don't relish the idea of talking about my parents at this precise moment in time.

"I'm a jealous man, Natalie," he says, and I can't help but let out a chuckle.

"And I'm a jealous woman, Jesse. Jesus, if you're going to put an argument forward for this to stop, make it a good one instead of half-assed excuses. Remember, you teach me how to argue, Professor, and I'm fucking good at arguing. Now, you think on that for a few whilst I do this..." Before he can say another word, I've slid down the wall and am crouching as I take him in my mouth.

"Fuck," he says as I move my head, licking, sucking, taking everything he's got to give.

I grab hold of his hips as I deep-throat him before he growls, one of his hands going to the back of my head, his fingers tangling in my hair. His eyes look into mine and I wink before moving faster, my hand coming back around and massaging his balls.

One... Two... Three... He moans and then unloads in my mouth. I swallow all that he gives and then stand back up, wiping my mouth with the back of my hand before he has me pinned back against the wall.

"I'm not good enough for you," he says, his eyes boring into mine.

"Says who?"

"Me."

"And who the hell are you to judge who is good enough for me?" I say.

"You know that this isn't a good idea, Natalie."

"Not really what a lady wants to hear after they've had your cock in their mouth," I say sarcastically. "I told you, if you're going to try and back away from this, then come up with a better argument, Jesse, because I don't scare easy."

"I'm not trying to scare you, I'm just—"

"Being a pussy. I don't need a pussy, I need a man," I say, my eyes blazing at him. "Fucking own your shit, Jesse."

He takes a moment, looking deep into my eyes, his jaw ticking before he speaks. "Fuck, I love the way you say my name."

"Yeah?" I say as I move my face closer to him, my lips hovering just over his before I move them to his ear. "It'll sound even better when you're inside me, and I can scream it out loud." I then duck down and under his arm, moving around him and to his office door, picking my bag up off the floor and slinging it over my shoulder as I go.

"You're going to be the death of me," he says, and I turn my head to look at him.

"Be a great way to die though, won't it?" I say with a wink before opening the door and sauntering out.

CHAPTER FOUR

"HEY, BABY DOLL," SAYS Drake as he sidles up next to me, slinging his arm around my shoulders and pulling me in close.

"Ugh, Drake, get off of me," I say as I push his arm off and walk a little bit faster.

"Come on, Nat, you can't resist my charms forever," he says, a stupid smirk gracing his face.

"No?"

"Nah, you'll give in eventually. Every girl wants a piece of this," he says as he grabs his crotch and thrusts forwards, his mates laughing behind him.

"Ah, there's your first mistake," I begin, stopping and turning to face him. He would be good-looking if he wasn't such an arrogant bastard. It's my biggest turn-off, arrogance. I have no time for people who think they are automatically entitled to something because they believe they are above everybody else. My parents may have a shitload of money, but they taught me right from wrong, they showed me how to be humble and realise that money just buys you expensive, materialistic shit that ultimately isn't worth a dime. Self-worth is more important, but I guess Drake never got the memo. "I'm a fucking woman, Drake, not a girl."

"Oh, I bet," he says, smiling, his eyes roaming up and down my body. I hide the shudder that convulses through me. Fucking creep.

"Your second mistake is thinking that I'm not already getting dick elsewhere."

"Pfft," he scoffs but his smile starts to fade as his friend's snigger.

"And your third mistake is forgetting that not only can I kick your ass, but so can my dad." I nod my head in the direction of my father, who stands a few feet away from us, his eyes menacing and his stance dominating the fucking moment. "So, if you wanna take the chance and keep pissing me off, which in turn pisses my dad off, then please, continue your pathetic display while you puff out your chest like a peacock, thinking you're the baddest thing since The Godfather."

"You and your dad ain't gonna do shit," he says, his smile gone and a snarl in its place.

"If you believe that then you're a stupider motherfucker than I first thought." I grit my teeth, not backing down, not cowering from a boy that thinks he can intimidate people to do what the fuck he wants. I don't like to use my dad as a bargaining chip, but Drake is an annoying ass that just won't quit. He's been trying to get in my knickers since I started Uni, and let's just say that he doesn't like to be told no. I've heard a few stories floating around about what he gets up to, and I want no part of it.

"Your pretty boy antics and fake as fuck swagger may work on others, Drake, but they don't work on me. Now, run along and find someone else to bug," I finish, and he looks at me before his eyes sideswipe to my dad again, and I notice that not only is my dad stood there, but so is my Uncle Miles.

I see Drake gulp and he starts to back away, his friends no longer sniggering or laughing but standing there with wide eyes and a dumb as fuck look on their faces.

Drake comes from old money which has passed down through generations, and he holds a lot of clout because of who his family are, but it means nothing to me, especially as his family are nestled so deep in the government. He thinks he's untouchable, but there is no such thing. Everyone gets their comeuppance at some point, and I would love to see him get his.

I have no doubt that Drake gets away with anything he does because of his standing, but one day, that standing won't mean shit. Most girls see his bleach-blond hair, his perma-tan that can only be achieved by a sunbed, his fast car and his designer get-ups. Doesn't take a genius to figure out he's loaded.

His group of assholes follow him as he skulks away, and I turn my attention to my dad and Uncle Miles.

"Hi, Dad," I say when I reach him.

"Hi, sweetheart," he says as he gives me a quick hug.

"What, no hug for your favourite uncle?" Uncle Miles interrupts, making me laugh. I pull away from my dad and hug Uncle Miles. "Who's the asshole?" he says when he breaks away from me, nodding his head in the direction of Drake.

"He's nothing I can't handle," I reply.

"That a girl," Uncle Miles says as he ruffles my hair.

"Will you quit doing that? I'm not five," I say, my words not sounding very serious considering I'm laughing.

"I don't care how old you are, my role in this life is to be your annoying-but-cool-as-fuck uncle."

"Language," my dad says, giving Uncle Miles a stern look. Uncle Miles just rolls his eyes and gives me a wink before walking over to my dad's car and getting in.

"So, now that your uncle has gone, what's the deal with Drake?" my dad asks, knowing full well who Drake is.

"He's just being Drake. I can handle him, Dad, don't stress," I say, trying to reassure my overprotective father.

"You know I can have him killed, right?"

I laugh. "Yes, Dad, I know." I may laugh, but I know my dad isn't messing around.

"Good. Just say the word and it's done," he says, all serious and shit.

"Got it. Now, you gonna tell me why you and Uncle Miles are here?" I ask, because they don't usually just appear at my Uni for no reason.

"Can a father not come and see his baby girl for no reason?" he says.

"No, he can't, now spit it out, Dad."

"Christ, you're just like your mother," he says, but he says it with nothing but affection.

"Want me to tell Mum you said that?" I say playfully.

"Natalie, you can tell your mother what you like," he says as if it's no big deal.

"She'd kick your ass."

"Maybe, but she loves me," he says.

I roll my eyes. "Okay, get to the point, Dad, what's up?"

"I need to make an appointment to meet with your Professors."

"What? Why?" I say too quickly.

He surveys me for a moment. "Why so cagey?"

"I'm not cagey," I say, and I know it sounds ridiculous as soon as the words are out of my mouth. "I just don't see why you need to make an appointment when my studies are fine, and not to mention that I'm going to be twenty next month, Dad. You know, I'm not a kid anymore."

He wouldn't even get an appointment, would he? I mean, what parent makes an appointment at a Uni for a nearly-twenty-year-old? Ugh, who am I kidding, my dad would totally do that, and because of who he is, he will get a fucking appointment.

"You'll always be my baby girl."

"I know that, but come on, please let me do this on my own, and if I need help, I will come to you and ask for your help." I stick my ground because my studies are fine whether I'm fucking one of the professors or not. "Does Mum know you're here?" I say, narrowing my eyes.

He looks away from me and I fling my hands into the air in exasperation. "Ugh, I knew it," I say, tapping my foot and folding my arms across my chest.

"Okay, fine, she doesn't know because she previously told me not to interfere unless you asked me to."

"So you decided to ignore her and interfere anyway," I say sarcastically. "She's gonna kick your ass when I tell her."

"You wouldn't."

"You know damn well that I would."

"Of course, you're your mother's daughter."

I smile, knowing that I have won this battle, for now.

"I won't tell her... As long as you promise to stop."

"Fine," he says begrudgingly. "Why did you have to grow up again?"

I stick my tongue out at him and he starts laughing.

"I'll see you at home later," he says before kissing the top of my head and getting into his car. I wave as he roars away with Uncle Miles.

If that little conversation taught me anything, it's to handle my reactions better at the mention of my professors. If I keep acting like there is something wrong, then they will pick up on it. I may be able to sweet-talk my dad, but my mum is another challenge entirely.

She wasn't the queen of the underworld for nothing.

CHAPTER FIVE

A LOT OF PEOPLE live their life the way they think they should. They conform to others, do what they think others would want and sacrifice what they actually want to do.

I make no apologies for knowing my own mind.

I make no excuses as to why I act the way that I do.

I've always been made aware of showing compassion to others, to help those that we love, but I've also been taught to never put someone else's wants and needs before my own. And I guess that's why I have no shame in walking to Jesse's office for the third time this week, because it's what I want to do.

Your path progresses at the speed that you choose, and I choose the fast lane. Always.

I enter his office and take a seat on the opposite side of his desk as he sits there, leant back in his chair, his eyes focussed on me.

"To what do I owe the pleasure?" he says, a hint of a smile lurking on his lips.

"I want to talk," I say firmly.

"Okay. Go on."

"At the risk of sounding like a fucking student, I need to know if this is just about sex for you?" I don't dance around the issue; I need to know. As much as I let lust take over me for the last two days, I want to get a sense of where this is going. I've been wanting this guy for the last three months... Actually, for the last year, but he's only been my professor for the last three months as his course isn't designed for first years, so I had only ever admired him from afar, until now.

"Do you honestly think that I would risk my career for a fuck?" he says, and damn if his tone doesn't have me feeling wet.

"I would like to think that an intelligent man like you would know his own mind, but you're still a guy with a dick, so I have to ask."

"I told you that once we crossed that line, there was no going back."

"And yet they are just words."

"Words that I don't take lightly." His stare penetrates me, and if I were a lesser woman then I would probably back down and let him have his wicked way with me. But I'm not a lesser woman, and I'll be damned if I'm going to let him talk me down this easily.

"You need to show me."

"And how am I supposed to do that, Natalie? Pull up to your house and knock on the door? Walk out of this office with you hand-in-hand? Shout from the rooftops that I've given into desires that have plagued me for months?" His words hit me deep.

Months?

He's wanted me for months?

"What do you mean months?" I ask.

"The first day I noticed you was when you were walking outside, laughing with your friends, looking carefree and like you were loving life. Your friend said something, and you turned your head, and that's when your eyes met mine."

I remember the moment he's talking about. I'd been on campus for about three months and I'd never seen him before. But the moment that I did, I knew that I wanted him.

"I'd never seen eyes like yours before. Stormy grey with a hint of silver." He closes his eyes as if he is watching the moment on replay in his mind. "I felt wrong for looking at you, but I couldn't stop. You smiled and that was when I knew."

"When you knew what?" I ask.

"When I knew that I would never be the same, that I would question every moral I had ever had. I've tried to push away what I feel when I'm around you, what I feel when I'm talking to you or answering your questions. I've tried so fucking hard to be a decent guy, but then there you were, on my desk, legs spread and waiting for me to claim you."

I take in a deep breath at his words, letting them flow over me, allowing the lust to work through me.

"And when you touched yourself, I knew that I would cross that line, that I would never be the man that I once was. I allowed my needs to take over, and now, I couldn't ignore what I feel if I tried."

"And what is it that you feel now?" I whisper.

"Natalie Valentine, I feel so much more than I could ever explain to you."

"Try," I urge, wanting him to tell me everything.

"I am a thirty-four-year-old man, and I've let my heart be captured by a nineteen-year-old student because we have no control over who our heart desires, and I have no fucking plans to let you go."

"I'm not a possession," I say, even though every part of me melts at his words.

"I know, and I would never want you to be. I know that you will challenge me, I know that you will push my boundaries, I know that I am risking everything to be with you, but this isn't just about getting my dick wet, Natalie.

"And now I ask you the same question. Is this just a fuck for you? A naughty romp with your professor? Something to brag about with your friends?"

"How fucking dare you," I say as I shoot up from my seat, hands on my hips. "One, I haven't told anyone about us... Two, no, this is not just some naughty romp... And three, I don't put it about, so no, this is not just a fuck."

"That fire, that passion that you have inside of you does things to me, Natalie, but answer me this... What happens when others find out? What happens when you look back in a few weeks and realise you made a mistake? What happens when you realise that I am too old for you and you want to be with someone your own age?"

"And what happens when you think that I am too young for you? What happens if you decide to kick me to the curb?" I counter. Two can play at that game, and I got a question for every single one that he drops my way.

He moves around the desk until he is stood in front of me.

"There will be people waiting to rip us to pieces because of what we have done. There will be those that want to break us and ruin our lives in the process. Are you telling me that you want a full-blown relationship with that amount of danger? A relationship that we have to keep quiet until you leave Uni, and it is deemed acceptable for us to be together?"

"Yes, to all of the above," I reply firmly, adamantly.

"Are you ready to fight, Natalie? Because whatever happens from here, we are going to have to fight."

"I was born to fight, Jesse, don't underestimate me."

"I don't."

"Good."

"So, this is it? We're really doing this?" he says.

"We already were," I reply before I move and place my lips on his.

Except this time, it's not rushed.

This time, it's not frenzied.

No. This time it's soft, sensual, and dare I say... a little romantic.

I push my body against his and place my hands on his firm, hard chest.

He envelopes me in his embrace, and it feels so right.

We are meant to be together.

I know it.

He knows it.

And now we just have to bide our time until the rest of the world knows it.

CHAPTER SIX

"DID YOU SEE HOW the fucker squirmed?" Uncle Miles says as I walk into the kitchen.

"Who you talking about?" I ask, intrigued as to who Uncle Miles has scared the shit out of now.

"No one," my dad says, giving Uncle Miles a stern look.

I narrow my eyes suspiciously. I'm not under any illusions when it comes to my dangerous family, but this feels different… like it has something to do with me.

"Uncle Miles," I say as I stalk forward, my eyes going to slits as I stare him down. He may be a bad motherfucker, but much like my father, he can be putty in my hands.

Uncle Miles goes to open his mouth, but my dad stops him from saying any words.

"Don't," he warns Uncle Miles who proceeds to shut his mouth and avoid eye contact with me.

I place my hands on the kitchen island and fixate my gaze on my dad. "Dad, what did you do?"

He stares me down, much like I'm doing to him. Pretty fucking obvious where I got my stubbornness from.

"Nothing that concerns you," he says, trying to act all nonchalant and shit.

"Bollocks."

"Don't speak to me like that, Natalie," he says, eyes blazing. He hates it when I swear at him or around him, and usually I keep it toned down, but on this occasion, I'm pretty sure I'm going to be saying a whole lot more once he finally tells me what him and Miles have been up to.

"Just fucking tell her, Joey," Uncle Miles says, and I swear, if he wasn't my uncle and my dad's friend, he would be getting punched in the face right about now.

"Miles, I swear—"

"Don't even try and divert by threatening Uncle Miles, Dad. You know you would never follow through with your threat anyway," I say, making Uncle Miles laugh out loud. "I get that you're a legend in the underworld, but to me, you're just my dad, so if this has something to do with me, I have a right to know. Total trust."

"Damn, she's good, Joey, just like her mother," Uncle Miles says, smirking at me.

"Don't I fucking know it," my dad says quietly, but not quietly enough because I hear him loud and clear. He runs his hands through his dark hair which is peppered at the sides with a few flecks of grey. "We paid Drake's dad a visit."

"You what?" I screech, a little too girly even for my liking. "Why the hell would you do that?"

"Because he was being a dick to you earlier," Uncle Miles says, and I give him my best death stare.

"So? I told you that I had it handled," I say, directing my anger back at my dad.

"Don't give a shit. You're my daughter."

"Again, so?"

"So I will do whatever I feel is necessary to keep assholes

away from you," he says as if it's no big fucking deal, when it absolutely is.

"For fuck's sake, Dad."

"Language," he reminds me, even though he swore not two seconds ago.

"Do you think that I am incapable of looking out for myself?" I ask, exasperated by his need to protect me.

"Of course not."

"Then why can't you just let me handle my own shit?"

"Because."

I wait a beat to see if he will expand, but he stays silent, picking his coffee up and taking a sip.

"Because?" I ask.

"Because if anyone pisses you or your mother off, they immediately go on my shit list," he says.

I take a deep breath before speaking. "Dad, I get it, I really do, you have this incessant need to make sure that I'm safe, but sometimes you poke your nose in where it's not warranted. Now all you have done is prove to Drake that I can't deal with his shit on my own, which means I gotta start all over again showing assholes like him that I don't need anyone else fighting my battles for me."

I shake my head and sigh before turning my back on them both and walking from the room. Honestly, my dad infuriates me at times.

"You okay, baby?" my mum says as she comes out of the lounge to see me walking down the hallway with my head hanging low.

"Just peachy," I say sarcastically.

"Well, either a guy has pissed you off or your father has," she comments.

"Try the latter."

"What's he done this time?" she says as she folds her arms across her chest and gives me a knowing look.

"Got involved in shit that doesn't concern him."

"Figures. Wanna talk about it?" she asks, and I shake my head.

"Not really, I'm just going to go out for a bit and cool off."

"Okay, will you be gone long?"

"I don't know. I need to clear my head and thought I'd go and see Sophia."

"So I have plenty of time to kick your father's ass?" she says, tilting her head to the side.

I laugh. "Yeah, be my guest."

"It'll be my pleasure," she says, smiling as she walks past me and into the kitchen. "Ah, there you are," I hear her say. "Miles, fuck off, I need to talk to my husband."

"Oh, charming," I hear Uncle Miles says. "Get straight to the point why don't you?"

"You know me, Miles, never one to beat around the bush. Now scram, unless you want an ass kicking from me too?"

"Nah, I'm good," I hear Miles say as I hear the sound of his chair pushing back on the kitchen tiles. "You're on your own, buddy."

Miles comes into the hallway, chuckling to himself. "Your dad's in trouble," he says as he walks past me to the front door.

"Good, so he should be."

Miles laughs. "See you later, Paige junior." He winks before leaving, the door clicking shut behind him.

"Now," I hear my mum say. "You been up to no good, Joey?"

"Depends on what you heard?" he replies.

"Oh, baby, you know better than to dodge my questions."

"I'm not sure I do... I think I need a reminder of what happens when I dodge them."

"Sounds like a challenge, Valentine."

"You better fucking believe it."

"You need the viper to come out?"

"Fuck yes."

Ugh. I've heard enough. So much for my mum kicking his ass. Sounds more like a fucking romance novel than a telling off.

I quietly let myself out of the house and take my phone out of my pocket.

There's only one person I want to see right now, and it isn't Sophia.

CHAPTER SEVEN

Jesse

I'M GOING TO HELL.
Straight to the gates of Hades.
I'm going to burn for all eternity.
And I don't fucking care.
I've lost my goddamn mind. I must have. I have always been a man that abides by rules, never crossing lines that I shouldn't. Until now. Until her. Natalie Valentine.
Jesus fucking Christ, she's a goddamn Valentine.
I've heard of the Valentine's; I know what they are rumoured to have done and who they are rumoured to have taken down. I shouldn't know this, but I do, and all because my friend, Brody, runs for them. Well, not for them exactly because they got out of the game a long time ago, but he runs for their acquaintances, so he tells me all about them and what he knows of their history. He drinks at Club Valentine which Joey and Paige own. He's been invited to their parties, because he's a goddamn part of their crew. He's told me about

the time years ago when they took down some of the nastiest bastards in history. He's told me too much, things I shouldn't know, and here I am, fucking their daughter, and dare I say, catching feelings for their daughter.

I don't even know how he really got involved with them, he just happened to be making more money than ever one day, and he told me who they were and what he was doing. I shouldn't even be friends with him because him being a drug runner would seriously compromise my job as a professor, but who the hell am I to talk when I've violated every rule put in place to keep a professor from sleeping with one of their students.

I know what it will look like to other people.

Older guy, younger woman, they'll call me a pervert, say that I prey on vulnerable women, but it isn't like that, not by any stretch of the imagination.

I had always admired Natalie from afar. There is just something about her. When she walks into a room, she lights it up. When she smiles, she radiates confidence. When she laughs, she makes others want to laugh with her.

I thought admiring her was wrong, that there was something wrong with me.

I chastised myself, told myself to get a grip and stop fawning over my student.

But then she came to me.

On my desk.

No knickers on, her legs wide open and her smart mouth.

And fuck me, I was a goner.

You show me any bloke that wouldn't be.

Pussy in your face.

Yeah, there isn't a man alive who is turning that down without serious thought.

I tried to. I really did, but then she touched herself, and fuck if that wasn't the sexiest thing that I had ever seen.

But it isn't just about sex.

She's smart, witty, funny, and can run rings around any woman my age.

If I had met her in a bar, on a dance floor, it would be different. I wouldn't have thought twice. It would have been normal.

I understand that there is an age difference, and I've tried to make her realise that she may not feel the same way in a few weeks, months, even years' time. But she's stubborn and she has her own mind. And I love that about her.

Love.

I'm not far away from it.

My feelings for her run deep.

It hasn't taken long for my heart to invest itself in our relationship. Because that's what we have. A relationship. And I wouldn't have put my whole fucking life on the line for anything other than love.

We can't choose who we fall for, and my chance may never come again.

So I'm going to own it.

I'm going to see if our relationship can be everything that I've dreamed of.

And if it isn't, then I just have to try and not get too burnt in the process.

CHAPTER EIGHT

Natalie

"HI," I SAY WHEN he answers the door.

"Hi," he says before he steps back and gestures for me to enter.

I smirk and move forwards, taking my first step inside a forbidden lair. It feels good, like I am meant to be here.

He closes the door behind me, and I look around. He lives in a modest house, cream walls, cream carpet lining the hallway, a few pictures hung up, a door to the right, a door at the end and a staircase to my left. Low lighting gives a comforting warmth, and I immediately feel at ease.

I probably shouldn't be feeling this way seeing as I am overstepping so many boundaries, but I do, and there isn't anyone in the world that can make me feel anything other than content right now.

I'm in his world, not mine.

I'm here of my own choices, not anyone else's.

I feel him step closer behind me and I close my eyes

briefly, allowing his scent to fill my senses. He smells good; his cologne is delicious, woody and sweet at the same time.

His hands find their way to either side of my hips, and I ignite inside from the contact. I never realised that feelings could be so powerful. One touch, that's all it takes for me to want to declare my love for him and plunge headfirst into whatever shitstorm our relationship is going to create.

I know he isn't just in this for sex.

It's about so much more than that.

His hand moves up my body until it's at my neck and pushing my hair away before his lips connect with my skin. I tilt my head to the side, elongating my neck, needing to feel more.

His lips are the best thing I've ever felt, and fireworks explode inside of me as he places light kisses on my skin.

"We could get into so much trouble for this," he says between kisses, but I fail to give a fuck about getting into trouble.

"You mean more trouble than if we got caught fucking on your desk at Uni?" I reply, a soft moan leaving my lips as he nibbles on my earlobe.

His tongue darts out and then he's turning me round, pushing me against the wall and holding my hands above my head.

"So much trouble... But when it comes to you, I'm prepared for it all," he says, his eyes holding mine and reaching my soul. "When I'm with you, it's like nothing and no one else exists."

"Laying it all on the line, huh, Professor?" I whisper, because as much as I want to be the sassy woman that captured his eye, I'm quickly becoming someone that needs him to breathe. I'm not a needy person and I never have been, but he may be about to change all of that. Jesse Marks... my fucking game changer.

"Too much for you to handle?" he says as he brushes his lips across mine.

"Never," I say before I push my lips against his, swallowing the deep growl he omits. I tease him with my tongue, luring him, wanting him to fuck me hard and then take me slow.

I've always known what I have wanted out of life, and the genes I carry ensure that I don't stop until I get it.

And right now, all I want is Jesse fucking Marks.

He pushes his body against mine and I feel how hard he is, how much he wants me, and how much his kiss conveys all the fucking passion that he is feeling.

I wiggle my hands out of his grip and wrap them around his shoulders, enjoying the feel of his rippling muscles beneath my fingertips.

God, this man drives me crazy.

Everything about him makes me insane. His beauty, his ruggedness, his physique, his intellect, and the way he devours me, like he can't get enough. The feeling is more than mutual.

He lifts me up and I wrap my legs around his waist as he caresses my ass.

"I want you," I whisper as I break my lips from his.

"I'm here," he says, his breath sweeping over my lips as he rests his forehead against mine.

"I want to feel you inside of me, I want you to worship me, and I want you to make love to me, Jesse." His eyes hold mine as I let myself show just how much I want him. I want to be completely intimate with him, in feelings and in touch. Our encounters so far have been wild and naughty. I need more. I want more. I deserve more.

"Natalie, I have no desire to do anything other than worship you. This may seem fast, rushed and totally crazy, but what I feel deep inside of me can never be broken. Fuck our ages, fuck everything for now... It's just you and me, baby—"

I press my lips against his, cutting him off.

I don't need to hear anymore.

I feel everything he is saying.

I feel the way we zing when we're together.

I feel how my body reacts to him.

I experience it daily, and it's intensified even more since we started this.

He starts to walk with me attached to him, my legs still around his waist as he starts to climb the stairs. He walks us down a hallway and through a door at the end. I allow myself a second to glance around and see we're in a bedroom decorated in blue with grey furnishings.

Jesse walks us to the bed and then slowly lowers me down until my ass touches the soft duvet. I put my hands behind me so that I can lean back as Jesse starts to unbutton his shirt. I admire every single thing that he does until he's completely stripped down in front of me. Laid bare with nothing to hide.

I lick my lips and sit forward, running my hands from my neck to the bottom of my tight-fitting T-shirt. I lift it up and over my head, throwing it to the side before standing up and kicking my heels off. I unzip my skinny jeans and push them down my legs, along with my lacy knickers and step out of them.

Standing upright, I reach behind me and unclasp my bra, letting it drop to the floor.

The whole time Jesse watches me, the heat building in his eyes with every single one of my movements. But this heat looks different. It's not just the wild wanting that I've seen from him before. There's more. Something else. Something deeper, and it makes my heart flutter.

He pushes me down and I drop to the bed, him following

until I am flat on my back and he is above me, his arms braced either side of me, his chest flush with mine.

"Make love to me, Jesse," I whisper, the air around us filled with sexual tension and a whole host of other indescribable feelings.

"This isn't just about sex for me, Natalie." He holds my gaze, his eyes conveying nothing but truth.

"I know."

Nothing else is said as he kisses me, pushing himself at my opening and sliding in deep.

He moves in and out slowly, continues to kiss me tenderly and makes me feel like I am his whole world.

Soft moans get swallowed by him.

My body feels every single touch like my senses have been heightened.

He rides me, takes me to the hilt, kisses me until my lips feel deliciously bruised.

His hands tangle in my hair, his thumbs brush my cheeks, his breath feathers my face.

With my legs wrapped around him, I come hard; harder than I ever have before.

I close my eyes, allow myself to enjoy every single minute of our combined release.

His guttural groan comes from deep within and arouses something inside of me.

I'm not sure what, but it's intense, like he has a grip on my heart, and it's frightened to let go.

We rock together, coming down from our highs.

And when he settles between my legs, he kisses my neck, my cheeks, making me want him to make love to me all over again.

I can't get enough of him.

I don't want to be without him.

It's been a week and I'm in so fucking deep I don't think

that I will ever see a way out, and I don't fucking want to either.

Jesse moves off of me and lifts me up, carrying me out of the bedroom and through a door on the right so we enter a bathroom.

He turns the shower on and waits a beat for it to warm up before he steps in and gently lowers my legs.

We stand together under the shower, the water cascading down on us and he worships me all over again.

CHAPTER NINE

Jesse

I STARE AT THE CEILING, Natalie lying on my chest, her hand splayed across my pec and my arm locked around her. Her hair fans out around her and her leg is hooked over mine.
Contented bliss.
Totally at ease.
Basking in the glow of what we just did.
Made love.
Not just a good hard shag, but a sensual, loving tryst.
I'm not a soppy shit, but damn, she's got me in knots.
Her beauty, her strength, her heart.
There isn't anything about her that I would change, not even her age. Sure, her being older or me being a bit younger would make things ten times easier, but then, we wouldn't be who we are now.
The passion that has fuelled us is turning into more. Well, it is for me.

I know that I'm going to fall hard for her, I just pray that she is there to catch me when I hurtle to the ground.

"What are you thinking?" she asks quietly as she starts to trail her fingers up and down my pec. It's nice, it's soothing.

"I don't think you really want to know."

She stops moving her fingers and props herself up on her elbow, so she is looking straight at me. Her long blond hair flows down her back, begging for me to run my fingers through it and then wrap it around my hand as I make love to her from behind, taking her slow, riding her deep.

"Come on, tell me," she says as she flashes her captivating silver-coloured eyes at me.

"If I tell you, it will either scare you or possibly make you think less of me," I say with a sigh.

"Scare me? You do know me, right?" she says with amusement in her tone.

"I'm well aware of the fact that I'm going to be running for my life when the word spreads about us," I reply, keeping my tone light so as not to ruin the post-orgasmic state that we are both experiencing.

"Stop dithering and just tell me," she says, unperturbed by the fact that her parents may very well kill me for touching their daughter.

"You're not going to let it go, are you?" I ask, even though I already know the answer.

"No, so you may as well get a move on and stop dragging it out."

"Fine," I say before taking a deep breath and letting it out slowly. "I know that we've only been doing this for a week—"

"Doing this?" she says, cutting me off, her eyebrows raised, her eyes slightly wide. "And what exactly is *this*?"

"Us. Together. In a relationship."

"That's better," she says, seeming satisfied by my answer.

I forge ahead with what I have to say. "I can't help the way

I'm feeling, Natalie, and I'm feeling more than I should be. What you do to me is something I've never experienced before. How you make me feel... You're like a drug, Natalie. My drug. My Natalie. And I know that my heart is quickly falling in love with you."

There. I said it. I actually voiced the words that will probably have her running for the fucking hills and have me left in the gutter, where I probably belong for getting involved with her anyway.

I wait.

I watch.

She says nothing.

My heart rate speeds up a little.

I'm left hanging, wondering what she is going to do next.

But I don't have to wait long as her hand glides down my body until it reaches my cock, her fingers wrapping around it and me instantly hardening beneath her touch.

She strokes me, up and down, slowly, gently before tightening her hold a little and then releasing it, over and over again.

My mind is all over the fucking place as she pleasures me, saying nothing about what I just told her.

I don't know what she feels, but it's clear she isn't about to run out of here.

No. She's far from running as she moves herself up until she is straddling me, her hovering over my cock, letting me feel her pussy on the tip.

"If it's not clear by now, Jesse, I'm not fucking scared, and I don't think any less of you. In fact, I feel more fucking turned on than I ever have done in my life." She sinks down a little, my cock nudging at her entrance, her warmth enticing me, making me want to spear myself inside of her and hit her deep.

"We are meant to be, Jesse, and I already know that once

I fall, I'm never getting back up." Those are her last words before she drops down on me, plunging my dick inside of her. She moans, I hold her hips, and she rides me like the world is about to end. Desperation takes over as she moves her hips faster, rolling them, holding her perfect tits with her hands, tweaking her nipples, letting me watch as she quickly starts to come apart. My fingers bite into her skin, she throws her head back, her hair touches my thighs, her back arches.

"So. Fucking. Beautiful," I growl.

She is.

Beyond beautiful. Breath-takingly so.

"And all fucking mine," I say with passion as she explodes around me, her cries ringing out, her pussy clenching around me. I manage to sit up, my arms going around her as I roar with my release.

It's powerful and all-consuming as we ride it out for as long as we can.

And then we collapse back onto the bed, her on top of me.

Our panting fills the room.

Our hearts race together as one.

And we both fall asleep as tiredness takes over, the memory of our lovemaking forever burned into our hearts.

CHAPTER TEN

Natalie

"WHAT TIME DO YOU CALL THIS?" my dad says as I stroll through the front door at two a.m.

I roll my eyes because I am nineteen—nearly twenty—and my dad still feels the need to wait up for me.

"Don't roll your eyes at me, young lady," he scolds. Ugh, I hate it when he says, "young lady." Makes me sound about five fucking years old.

"Dad, please, I'm an adult and I can come in at whatever time I like."

"Is that right?"

"Yes. You and Mum have made sure that I am responsible, so why do you feel the need to question me?"

"Because I can."

"Pfft." I blow a lock of hair out of my face in frustration. I know his word is law everywhere, but with me, I need him to give me some room to just be myself. "I'm not one of your crew, Dad, I don't need you to keep tabs on me, and I don't need to answer to you all the damn time."

"Like fuck you don't," he says, and I can hear the annoyance in his voice. "And you are most certainly one of my crew because you're a Valentine. You will always be one of my crew."

"You know what I mean, Dad. I'm not someone that you need to keep watch over."

"If you believe that, Natalie, then you're just kidding yourself. I may not be in the game anymore, but there will always be assholes out there waiting to try and hurt me. I've done some shady shit in my lifetime, and yes, I only did it to those who deserved it, but I would die before I let anyone use you to hurt me."

It's always been a fear of his. He's always been overprotective, ready to take anyone out that dares to try and trample all over me. But he's way off the mark. I don't need protecting, not now, not ever. I'm not my mother's daughter for nothing. I have my mum's fire, something both her and my dad have told me more than once.

"Dad, I know you worry, but I am sensible, and I would absolutely come to you if I needed your help," I say, trying to tame his anxiety when it comes to me.

"And I'm pleased to hear it, but it doesn't explain where you have been until two in the goddamn morning," he says, and I know that he isn't going to back down.

"I told you that I was going out to see Sophia."

"Except... You didn't see Sophia, did you?" he says with one eyebrow raised, and I know that I am fucked. If he knows that I wasn't with Sophia, then he is going to want an explanation as to why I lied.

Fuck.

Quick, Natalie, think.

"Okay, please don't be mad…" I start and I instantly know I've used the wrong opener here.

"Not really the way you want to start this conversation," my dad says as he folds his arms across his chest.

I sigh and admit defeat. I'm going to have to tell him something, he's going to know that I've been with a guy, it's bloody obvious. Why else would I be out until two?

I am about to open my mouth and tell him that I've been chilling with some guy from Uni, but my mum's voice stops me from uttering another word.

"Joey, what the hell are you doing?" she says as she marches down the stairs, her silk dressing gown wrapped around her, her long blond hair flowing down her back. My mum always looks immaculate, whether she has herself dolled up or not. She doesn't need to doll her herself up either, she's always beautiful.

"I'm asking our daughter where the hell she has been tonight," he answers, turning to look at my mum who comes to a stop in front of him, hands on her hips and one foot tapping the floor.

"For fuck's sake, Joey, go to bed," she says, her tone determined, fierce.

"Pardon?"

"Go. To. Bed. Stop interrogating Natalie and realise that she's an adult who doesn't need your permission to leave this house."

I want to hug my mum and give her a high-five for rescuing me from having to lie to my dad again.

"Two in the morning, Paige. Two in the fucking morning."

"Yes, I'm fully aware of the time," my mum replies, not batting an eyelid at my dad's tone.

"She wasn't with Sophia either."

"So?"

"So, she lied to us, Paige."

"I'm not condoning the lying, but come on, baby, you're not exactly the most mellow person in the world." I snicker at my mum's comment and it instantly earns me a scowl from my dad.

"And what is that supposed to mean?" he asks, even though he knows he's a pain in the ass sometimes.

"I don't need to spell it out to you, Joey, because you're not stupid and we haven't just got together. No blinkers, baby."

My dad sighs.

"Go back to bed and I'll deal with Natalie," my mum says as she looks at me, and I suddenly don't know whose wrath I would prefer.

My dad stands on the spot for a tense few seconds before conceding defeat and kissing my mum on her forehead before walking up the stairs. He doesn't say another word to me, and he doesn't turn back around. I instantly feel bad that I made him worry.

When my dad disappears completely, my mum turns her full attention to me.

"I don't want to talk about this now, Natalie, but just know that I will expect answers in the morning," she says before going back up the stairs and leaving me rooted to the spot.

Fuck. I need to come up with a damn good excuse. My mum can sniff out a bullshitter from a mile away.

I walk up the stairs, my shoulders drooped and my head hanging low.

There is no way in hell that I am telling them about Jesse, so I need to come up with a believable alternative, and quick.

I'M ALREADY UP and dressed by the time my mum walks into the kitchen.

It's a Sunday morning, and I'm usually still in my pit at nine a.m., but today I need to do some damage control before my parents freak out and have a fucking surveillance team on my ass.

"Morning," I ring out, a little too cheerfully for my usual morning grumpiness. Yes, I am that person that needs to drink her coffee in peace and be left to my own devices until the caffeine kicks in and I can attempt human conversation.

"Good morning," my mum says as she takes a seat at the kitchen island.

"Coffee?" I ask as I get up from my stool and go to the coffee machine.

"Please."

Silence engulfs us as I busy myself making a drink for my mum and try to keep my nerves at bay. I'm not usually a nervous person, hell, I opened my goddamn legs on a desk for my professor, so I think we can assume that I am normally packing a shit load of confidence. But this morning, not so much.

I take my mum her drink, placing it in front of her before sitting back on my stool.

My mum sips her coffee, keeping me waiting a little bit longer. She is the fucking master of dragging shit out, making you more and more nervous as the seconds tick by.

"Delicious coffee," she says as she puts the cup back down and wraps her hands around it. She is looking every inch the boss lady that she is, dressed in her designer trouser suit with a crisp white shirt underneath. I presume she's going into the club today... Either that or she's off to kick someone's ass. Maybe mine? I don't fucking know.

"I made a fruit salad in the fridge," I tell her, attempting to keep my voice even.

"I'm okay for now," she says as she continues to watch me. "You know, Natalie, you may be my daughter, and I may let things slide with you because of that, but I can see how nervous you are... And I guess, my first question is, why? Why do you look like you want the ground to swallow you up?"

Oh boy. I take a deep breath and try to push the nerves away that flutter inside of me.

"I just... I don't want you and Dad to make a big deal about me being out so late last night. I am a grown-ass woman."

"I know that, but it's our job to worry about you, no matter how grown-ass you might be," she replies with one eyebrow raised.

"I get it, I do... But what are you going to do when I leave home and get my own place? You gonna put tabs on me? Stick a fucking chip underneath my skin?"

"Hmm... Maybe don't tell your father about the chip idea," she says with a smile.

"He wouldn't."

"He absolutely fucking would, and you know it," she says, and I know that she's right. "He only wants to protect you, as do I."

"I know, Mum, but come on, you can't expect me to divulge every aspect of my life. I need my freedom, and I need to feel like I don't have a leash around my neck."

"A little bit dramatic, Natalie," she says as she takes another sip of her coffee.

I roll my eyes in response.

"Look, I don't need you to tell me that you were with a guy last night, and neither does your father. It's plainly obvious. But what isn't obvious is why you lied. That is the part that we're having trouble dealing with." She looks a little hurt that I lied to them and that goddamn guilt rises up inside of me. I've always been close to both of my parents, and we've always been honest, so I've really gone and upset the apple cart by telling a big fat fib.

"I just don't want Dad going all crazy," I say, being as honest as I can.

"Your Dad isn't stupid, Natalie, and he would only go crazy if there was a need for it," she says, and I raise my eyebrows at her which makes her chuckle. "Okay, okay, so he can go a little overboard—"

"Understatement of the year."

She ignores my comment and continues speaking. "Listen, we've never hidden who we are from you. Of course we haven't gone into detail about some of the stuff we've done, but we've always been truthful with you. You know the world we live in and the circles we run in. We may have handed our crowns to your Aunt Meghan and Uncle Miles years ago, but we are still very much involved in the way they operate. We have enemies, Natalie, and we always will have because others don't like the power that we still hold.

"We all just want you to be happy and safe, and unfortunately, there is always going to be an element of danger to your life because of who we are. Being a Valentine is something others dream of, but it does have its cons. I wouldn't trade any of what I have been through because I love your father and I love what we have together, but you must remember that we haven't had easy paths. We've had to work hard to protect ourselves, and we will always work hard to protect you."

"But I don't need protecting, I know what I'm doing," I argue.

"Do you?" she questions.

"Yes, Mum," I say with a sigh before I move off of my chair and go to stand beside her. "I appreciate all you do for me, and I know that you have done some shady shit in your past, but I'm okay. I am happy, I am safe, and I am truly sorry that I lied to you both. I would never want to hurt you because as crazy as you guys are, I love you."

"I love you too, baby girl," she says with a smile before adding, "But just answer me one thing. This guy... Is it serious?"

"Yes," I answer without hesitation.

"Will you tell me more when you figure out where it's going?"

"Of course I will, Mum."

"Okay," she says with a nod of head. "Don't lie to us again, Natalie." Her tone changes to one that is harder, a little more menacing.

"I won't."

"If you're going to see this guy, then just tell us that. I don't need a name yet because I trust your word when you say that you are safe, but just know that I will need more at some point and that isn't because I don't trust you but more because I am your mother, and I am interested in your life."

"Okay, Mum. Thank you," I say as I give her a hug. "You know you're the best mum, right?"

She chuckles. "Oh, I know, but also know that I am the best at kicking ass too."

"Yes, I know," I say with a laugh, and even though I am laughing, I absolutely know that it is the truth.

"Right, well, I better go and placate your father."

"Ewww." I screw up my nose and my mother laughs at me. "I'm going out."

"To see the guy?" she asks.

"Yes." He has no idea that I plan to visit him today, but I figure that it will be a good surprise.

"Okay. Have fun and let me know if you plan to come home for dinner."

"I will. Thanks, Mum," I say as I bounce from the room

and go to my bedroom to collect my handbag with everything I need inside of it.

Well, that went better than I thought it would... Maybe him being older won't be so much of an issue when my parents find out?

CHAPTER ELEVEN

Jesse

"You know what, Bruce, just drop it," I say as my best friend tries setting me up on a fucking blind date, again. Actually, I think it's more because his wife, Sasha, insists that I need to find somebody. She's been going on about it for years, and it always gets on my goddamn nerves, but it annoys me even more now because I have found someone... I just can't fucking tell anybody about it yet.

"Come on, Jesse, you have been out of the game for so long, and Sasha is being a pain in my ass about this," Bruce says, confirming what I already knew.

"So, this is just about keeping the wife happy, huh?"

"Of course, you moron. I couldn't give a shit what you do as long as you're happy. If you're fine being a one-man band and tugging to your own tune, who the hell am I to come in and fuck that up for you," he replies, and I can't help but laugh at his reference to me being a one-man band. If only he knew.

"Why does Sasha care so much about this?" I question for what feels like the millionth time.

"Because she cares. God knows why when all you have done is crap all over any blind date that she has set you up on."

"Hey, there was a reason for crapping on every single one, and that is plainly because the women weren't my type." That's putting it mildly. Between the woman with the common sense of a gnat and the one that thought it would be a great idea to show me her in-growing toenail in a restaurant full of people, it's enough to put you off for life. And it has done just that. I've been on about ten dates that Sasha set me up on, and each time I came back more miserable than before.

I've never been one to force the idea of a relationship with anyone, and to me, blind dates are a thing of horror. I could write a fucking book about the dating faux pas' that I have endured.

"So who is your type, Jesse? I've known you a long time, and apart from seeing you with two women, one of which was in college and fucking years ago, I don't even know what your type is."

"Are you fishing for me to tell you?" I ask because this isn't something Bruce would ordinarily ask me, and I can only presume that Sasha has put him up to this to help her set me up on another nightmare.

"Help me out here, buddy. The wife is home all day long, does lunch with her friends and has more time on her hands than she knows what to do with," he says with a sigh.

"You need to get her pregnant," I joke.

"Fuck no. I'm good with things as we are. Do you know I had to deal with a kid yesterday who thought it would be a good idea to throw a fucking pebble at the window, just to see if it smashed? I mean, common sense would tell you that it is going to fucking smash, surely?"

I can't help but laugh. "Being a teacher isn't exactly all it's cracked up to be, is it?"

"I don't know, your job seems easier than mine. At least you teach people who are already fucking adults, meanwhile I get to try and train a bunch of seven-year-olds who literally drive me insane by the end of the day."

"Christ, Bruce, you really make it sound like you hate your job," I comment, even though I know he doesn't hate it per se.

"I don't hate my job, I just find some of the kids frustrating because no matter what I do, they do not fucking listen. So, no, I have no plans to subject myself to having a kid anytime soon, and luckily, Sasha feels the same. She's quite happy with a tidy house, her freedom and being able to have sex whenever we feel like it instead of having a kid cock-block us until we're too old and past it to want to bother."

"I'll be sure to remember that," I say as his rant comes to an end.

"You don't need to worry, at this rate, your dick will be all shrivelled up and useless before you decide to settle down."

"Ha ha, you're hilarious," I reply dryly.

"I think so."

"Anyway, how do you know that I'm not seeing someone secretly?" I tell him, wanting him to wrap up this ridiculously pointless conversation.

He pauses for a beat. "Are you?"

"Maybe."

"Don't fuck about, Jesse, this could really get the lady off of my case," he says, and I'm sure I hear some form of excitement at the prospect of Sasha giving him a break about this.

"Yes, I am seeing someone, and, no, I'm not ready to

share anything other than that yet." It's as much as he is going to get out of me.

"Thank God for that. I'll be sure to tell Sasha, and finally she can move on and focus on setting up someone else who isn't my best friend."

"Does she really give you that much grief about this?" I know Sasha is like a dog with a bone when she gets an idea in her head, but damn, this just seems a little obsessive.

"Fuck yeah she does. Honestly, it's a good job I love her and worship the ground she walks on, otherwise I'd have been ready to throw in the towel a long time ago."

Huh. Doesn't exactly make married life sound very fun.

Bruce and Sasha have been together for eight years, married for five. I guess, after time, you must tend to look for other things to occupy your mind.

"Are you guys getting on okay?" I ask, because if he needs to talk, I'm here to lend an ear.

"Yeah, we're good, she just gets an idea and won't let go of it until she has seen it through to the end, you know that," he says with a sigh.

"I do know that." I nod even though he can't see me.

"Just don't keep it secret for too long, and I'm no chick, but I kinda wanna know who the woman is, dude."

"You're just as nosey as your wife," I say whilst laughing.

"I live vicariously through you," he banters back.

"Must have been pretty fucking boring up until now then," I reply, keeping the joke going.

"Yeah, you had me worried for a while, but I just want you to be happy, dude. I mean, unless you have to keep it secret because you're fucking a student." He roars with laughter and I have to force myself to laugh along with him, even though it pains me to do so. I get why he's taking the piss, but damn, it's too near the mark.

"I mean, I know your students are technically adults, but

can you imagine the shit you'd get? Oh my God, Sasha would lose her shit." He continues to laugh, and I have to swallow down the lump in my throat, forcing myself to keep fucking laughing along with him.

It doesn't feel right to laugh.

It's wrong, but what other choice do I have?

I hear a knock on the door, and I have never been so fucking thankful in my life.

"Bruce, I gotta go, there's someone at the door," I tell him.

"Probably your mystery lover, huh?"

"And you'll never know," I say before I hang up the phone and go to the door.

CHAPTER TWELVE

Natalie

He looks shocked when he opens the door, but he really shouldn't be seeing as I am not a woman to wait around, and he damn well knows it.

He knew it before we began this.

He saw the determination in me when we just had the student and teacher relationship going.

He knows I'm not going to wait for him to keep making the first move.

And I guess, it would be harder for him to make the first move because he has so much more to lose than I do.

I'm convinced more than ever that my parents will be okay with this. It may take some time, but they will see how happy Jesse Marks makes me, regardless of who he is.

"Natalie." His voice floats over me and ignites that fire that burns deep inside of me for him. My nipples pebble underneath my clothes, and my pussy clenches in anticipation of having his cock buried inside of me.

"Jesse," I say with a smirk. "You gonna invite me in?"

"Of course," he says as he steps back and gestures for me to enter. I do so and sway my hips as I pass him. He won't be able to see my ass properly because of the long coat I'm wearing, although I'm sure he will have me butt-naked in no time.

I turn and watch him close the front door, and then he stands there, his hands in the pockets of his black jogging bottoms. Dear fucking God. He looks delicious. His tight T-shirt shows me the ripples of his muscles and again I have to try and calm my overactive pussy down.

"So, this is a nice surprise," he says with a smile.

"Yeah?"

"Hell yeah."

"Well, it's about to get a whole lot better," I say as I unbutton my long coat and let it fall to the floor, along with my handbag which lands with a clump beside me.

I watch as Jesse's mouth hangs open, his eyes roaming up and down my lingerie-clad body.

Yes, that's right, I came dressed in nothing but my lingerie, my heels and my coat. Of course I have clothes in my larger-than-life handbag for when I leave later.

"Fuck me," Jesse says on a whisper.

"I plan to," I say before walking to him and placing a light kiss on his lips. He tastes of coffee, and not the shitty cheap brand stuff, more the expensive stuff that I have become accustomed to since I started needing a caffeine hit.

"Did you drive over here?" he asks.

"Yes."

"Dressed like that?"

"Yes."

"And what if you had been stopped?"

"Then I would have made sure not to flash anyone."

"You weren't worried about being caught dressed like this?"

"Not at all."

"You really give no fucks, do you?" he asks.

"None at all," I reply before smashing my mouth against his, smearing my red lipstick as I devour him, his tongue meeting mine stroke for stroke.

I move my hand to his dick and place it over his trousers, cupping him and squeezing him gently. He growls, I smile, and together we become a frenzied, tangled mess of limbs. We stumble backwards but don't make it any farther than a few steps before he smashes me against the wall, his mouth travelling down my neck until it reaches my breast. He licks, he sucks, he pulls down my lacy bra and sucks my nipples in turn as if he has never tasted anything so good before.

I grasp the back of his neck, pushing him against me, needing him to do more. I need more. I want more. I feel like I will not fucking breathe until he is buried inside of me, deep, penetrating and pounding into me like a sailor on leave.

He moves his lips lower, trailing them across my stomach and down to my lacy thong that doesn't hide much to be honest, but conceals just enough to make him want to rip the material from me. Which he does, throwing the scrap of material to the side.

"I'm yet to taste you, Natalie," he whispers, his breath hot over my bare pussy. I have to resist the urge to grab the back of his head and put his lips on the place that needs it the most right now. I'm throbbing with the fucking need for him to suck my damn clit.

He taps the inside of my thighs in turn with his finger.

"Spread them," he says, and I immediately comply, moving them to the sides, stretching myself as far as I can whilst still being able to hold myself up.

"That's better," he mumbles, and then I feel his tongue dart out and touch the tip of my clit. A shockwave pulses through me at the slight touch. Christ, I'm going to be a fucking mess by the time he actually buries his face in me.

I feel his hands go either side of my hips, and then his thumbs are pulling me apart, spreading me so I am on full display before him.

"Fucking beautiful," he says before he runs his tongue from the bottom of my slit and all the way to the top. He does that over and over again, and I feel like I am going to self-combust if he doesn't do more.

"Jesse, please," I pant.

He chuckles, the vibrations tingling on my skin. "You want more?"

"Yes."

"Then look at me," he says as I tilt my head forward and connect my eyes with his. "Watch as I make you come, Natalie."

And then he's licking me, sucking me just where I wanted him to.

I struggle to keep my eyes open, but my fascination of the way in which he works me into a frenzy keeps my adrenaline pumping so I can keep watching.

"Fuck, Jesse," I pant out as I feel my legs start to tremble. He doesn't answer me because he's too busy with his tongue, and then his finger is inside of me, pulsing in and out, slowly, deliciously. I've never been so fucking turned on in all my life... Or so I thought until Jesse moves his other hand to the back of me and spreads my ass cheeks.

I momentarily feel shocked as he sweeps his finger up and down, between my cheeks, his eyes watching me as he continues to tend to my throbbing clit.

"Jesse," I whisper, a little unnerved.

He takes his finger out of my pussy and then taps my right leg before gently helping me move my leg, so it drapes over his shoulder, stretching me in a different way, allowing his finger to brush between my cheeks easier before he is nudging against my opening and slowly inserting his finger in a place that has remained untouched, until now.

Oh my fucking God!

I feel like I'm going to faint.

The amount of pleasure that I am getting from this is indescribable.

I can't take it.

It's too much.

He sucks my clit harder, pushes his finger in deeper, and then I am fucking exploding, screaming out his name, struggling to hold myself up as I free-fall through the most powerful orgasm of my life.

"Jesus, Jesse," I say as I pant, trying to catch my breath. He doesn't let up as I turn to jelly, my legs losing their strength as I slide down the wall. He's still sucking my clit as I go from standing to crouching, his finger now removed from my ass. "Jesse, I can't... It's too much..."

I lose the ability to say another word as he rips his mouth away from me and pushes me to the floor before he mounts me and slams his cock inside of me.

I scream and feel him plunge deep.

His lips brush against mine and he growls fiercely, possessively.

My eyes connect with his, and I see the ferocious need inside of him... Need for me... Need for us.

I lift my arms and wrap them around the back of his neck, and I do the same with my legs, linking them around his waist, tilting my hips a little so he hits me even fucking deeper.

The amount of passion between us right now is second to none.

Intense.

Intimate.

All-consuming.

He pounds into me and I meet him each time, our flesh smacking together, echoing off the hallway walls.

His forehead comes to rest against mine and I can feel my walls tighten, clamping around him as I head towards another orgasm.

"You're mine, Natalie," he growls out.

"And you're mine, Jesse." Tit for tat.

"I fucking love you," he says and his words are my undoing as I hit the highest peak and convulse around him, squeezing him as he pounds harder into me.

"I love you too," I say and then it's his turn to lose control.

He roars, the sweat beading on his forehead.

And when he slows down, he allows us a moment to catch our breath before he places a kiss on the tip of my nose.

"Do you mean it?" he asks, and I place my hands on either side of his face as I look deep into his eyes.

"Every fucking word." I have never meant anything more.

"How did I get so lucky?" he whispers, now looking at me as if he can't believe his luck.

"Right place, right time?" I tease.

He doesn't tease back, instead keeping the intensity that we had a few seconds ago. "You're special, Natalie, and you're all mine."

"Yes I am."

"Fuck," he says before kissing me softly, his lips moving against mine.

This man.

He is it for me.

And I am it for him.

There are no rules when it comes to love.

And I love him.

It might seem fast, but I don't care.

There is no timeframe for what happens in our lives.

We just have to work with what we get given.

And I was given Jesse Marks, and I'm not ever letting him go.

CHAPTER THIRTEEN

Jesse

I'VE BEEN WALKING around struggling with a raging hard-on for most of the morning. I mean, I'm usually composed, but Natalie upped the stakes in bringing me to my fucking knees today.

She walked into class, dressed in a tartan mini-skirt, a white tank top, biker-chick boots and a fitted leather jacket, long silver chains hanging around her neck and dangling between her breasts, her long blond hair curled, her eye make-up more dramatic than usual. She sat at the front, her usual seat, and when the whole class was situated, ready to start the lecture, she opened her legs just enough to show me that she was going commando.

Mother of God.

She's brazen, forward, and she's all fucking mine.

So, when I see Drake talking to her outside as I make my way to the cafeteria to grab some lunch, it sets off a dominant need inside of me to drag him the fuck away from her and then throw her over my shoulder and take her into my office, like a goddamn caveman.

I fucking hate Drake. He stinks of money and he thinks that brings him all the power, like it's his God-given right to walk around the place like he owns it.

I've heard stories about Drake, and I have no doubt that they are true. He shows no shame, and I don't like him near my woman.

I walk slower, wanting to see if he leaves her alone. Her face is screwed up and she's looking at him like she wants to pummel his face in. That makes me feel a little better at least, but then his hand grabs the top of her arm and you can bet your ass that I am flying across the path until I am standing behind him. Natalie sees me, but she doesn't let on that I am here.

"You think you're so fucking special because you're a Valentine. Pfft, you ain't worth shit, Natalie. Not you or your fucking parents. I could ruin all of you, and all it would take is a click of my fingers."

"All of this because I don't want to get on my knees and suck your miniscule cock, Drake?" Natalie goads him, her eyes full of hate.

"Oh, you better believe that you would be fucking privileged to suck my cock, and one day, you'll be begging for me to stick it in you, and I'm going to enjoy every moment of taking you in the way that I want," he says, making me feel fucking sick with his disgusting threats.

"Do you want to repeat that, Drake?" I say, my voice hard.

He whirls around and I see him gulp.

"Professor Marks, I didn't realise—"

"Oh, I think it's very clear that you didn't realise anyone was listening, Drake. I'll be reporting this to the head, and if I ever hear of you threatening another student, I'll make sure that you never set foot inside this university again. Do I make myself clear?"

"Yes, sir," he says, like the little pussy that he really is. He can't hide behind money forever, and one day he will get his comeuppance.

"Good. Now, go," I say, my eyes boring into him as he walks away. I wish I were younger, because then I could actually punch the runt.

"You feel better now?" I hear Natalie ask, but I don't turn around to face her until Drake has disappeared from my sight.

"What the hell was that about?" I ask her.

"It was just Drake throwing his weight around as usual."

"He does this a lot?" I ask, wondering how many times he's put his hands on her.

She rolls her eyes and crosses her arms over her chest. "It's Drake, it's what he does, and he's pissed because my dad and uncle went to pay his dad a visit because they saw him bugging me last week."

"Why didn't you say anything?" I ask her.

"Because we hadn't even really figured out what we were at that point, and to be fair, you can't do anything because no one is allowed to know about us. If you start getting all up in my business then people will notice, and they will talk."

She's got a good point, and fuck if it doesn't infuriate me that I can't do more.

If only she wasn't a goddamn student.

If only I wasn't her professor.

I am pretty sure I'll be saying those words until the day she graduates... and maybe after then too because we can't come straight out and announce that we're a couple. Doing that would still require an investigation into when our relationship began, and the reality hits me like a freight train.

I stumble back a little, suddenly wondering what the fuck

I'm doing.

"Jesse, are you okay?" I hear Natalie ask me, and then her hand is brushing against my arm.

"Don't touch me where people can see," I grit out and instantly feel bad because she looks hurt by my words. "Fuck, I'm sorry, I didn't mean to snap."

"Then why did you?" she says as I watch her slip into defence mode.

"I just... I..." I run my hands through my hair and take a deep breath. "I'm just pissed about Drake."

She eyes me quizzically, like she doesn't believe me.

"I'll give you a piece of advice, Jesse... Don't ever fucking lie to me again." She turns and walks off, leaving me hanging and wishing that I had handled that conversation differently.

I glance around to see if anyone was watching us, but they're all too busy talking or eating their lunch as they walk around and find a spot to sit down.

Yesterday we were declaring our love for each other, and today she's mad at me, and I'm pissed at myself.

I haven't been in a relationship for a long time, but even I know that I have fucked up here. Lying is a big no-no, I should have just told her that I came to the realisation that we are going to have to hide what we are for a lot longer than I originally first thought.

I need to do damage control, and quick.

Natalie is not a woman that will take being lied to, no matter how small that lie may be.

I didn't even find out what actually happened between her dad and Drake's dad. I feel so out of the fucking loop that it is ridiculous.

I don't want to be on the outside looking in, only catching a glimpse when I am able to.

I've fallen hard and fast.

I can only hope that she has fallen as much as I have.

CHAPTER FOURTEEN

Natalie

Fucking men.

Who do they think they are?

Trying to intimidate me.

Thinking they can put their goddamn hands on me.

And worst of all, lying to me.

I mean, I expect the worst of Drake, fucking mummy's boy who can't deal with anything without the backing of his parents and their money.

But what I don't expect is Jesse to lie to me. I won't stand for it, and if he thinks that I am going to sit around whilst he is figuring out what he wants to say, then he's got another thing coming. I'm not some stupid little girl who will allow him to do that. I respect myself more than that, and he should respect me too.

I make my way to my car, just so I can sit and have a time out for a few minutes, but I don't make it that far as Sophia comes and steps into line beside me. I keep walking, and she quickens her pace.

"Jeez, who pissed you off?" she asks.

"Fucking Drake." I can't tell her that actually it's Jesse because then I would have to tell her the truth.

"Ugh. What's the douche done now?"

"Tried to intimidate me with empty threats of sticking his dick in my pussy."

"Oh, charming," she says sarcastically.

"Right? He doesn't seem to get that I can't fucking stand him," I fume.

"Oh, he gets it, but he sees you as a challenge," she says.

"Yeah, I know." Drake always goes for those who pose a challenge until he grinds them down or does some shady shit to get them on board, but he really did shit out when he set his sights on me.

"He makes my skin crawl," she says, and I agree with her.

"He's just a fuck boy that has a tantrum when he can't get his own way."

"Mmmhmm."

We walk in silence as I lap the field instead of going to my car like I had planned.

"You wanna go to Tulip this weekend? It's been forever since we went," Sophia says, and I think back to the last time we went out. I can't actually remember when it was. My mind is so focussed on Jesse that I can't think straight.

Tulip is the nightclub that everyone goes to on the weekends. It is the hot spot and where you will occasionally see the odd celebrity sitting in the VIP section. It's also owned by my Aunt Meghan and Uncle Miles and run by their son, Marshall, so I have a free pass to go there whenever I want, and of course I get the VIP treatment when I'm there.

"Friday night?" I ask her.

"Fuck yes," she replies, the excitement clear on her face and from her jumping up and down on the spot.

"Okay, okay, calm down, it's just dancing," I say whilst laughing.

"I don't care, it's been ages since we danced and did tequila shots."

"You're right, it has been too long since we let loose and had some fun."

"Well, your head seems to have been elsewhere for the last few weeks," Sophia comments.

"How so?"

"Well, you haven't been yourself, you've been absorbed in something, I just don't know what."

"That's ridiculous," I scoff. I've only been seeing Jesse for just over a week now, so her claim that I haven't been present is stupid.

"No it's not. You have this spaced-out look most of the time, like your mind is somewhere else even though you're physically present. You mentally check out on me, and I was starting to think that I had done something wrong," she says, and I stop walking, shocked that she feels like this.

"Sophia, you know that I would tell you if there was a problem," I say softly, wanting to put her mind at ease.

"That's what I thought, but really, think about the last time you called me or picked up my calls."

I think about it for a moment, and again I don't remember when I last spoke to her on the phone. We used to speak every couple of days even with seeing each other here, so it's weird that we haven't chatted by phone, and it's worrying that I hadn't even fucking noticed. Christ, I've become a woman that is obsessed with everything about a guy, and I always swore that I wouldn't become that person.

"I'm sorry," I say, feeling genuinely guilty that I haven't been there for her.

"It's okay, we all need our moments, just don't let your moment go on for too long, I miss you," she says, getting all soppy on my ass. Sophia is the sensitive one, and I pack the sass. It's always been that way. "And you know that you can talk to me about anything, right?"

"Of course," I say with a smile.

"Good." She smiles back at me and I feel like whatever the hell had shifted between us has returned back to how it was before. I need to think about more than Jesse and his magnificent dick. I have a life, and I won't revolve it around him.

Everyone gets to that stage in their relationship where they can't keep away from one another, and they can't focus on anything but each other, but I'm done with that. I need to be present in all other aspects of my life too.

This would be so much easier if people knew about us.

Roll on graduation. Only another six months to go and then he won't be my professor anymore. I will be moving on to the next stage of my degree, and luckily, Jesse doesn't teach the next part.

One day we can be a normal couple, it's just a case of being patient.

And it's also a case of him apologising and explaining to me why the fuck he lied.

CHAPTER FIFTEEN

Jesse

O<small>UT OF ALL</small> of the women that I could have fallen in love with, it had to be a woman that was forbidden, and one that would have me crawling on my knees, begging for forgiveness.

That is me right now.

In my office.

On my knees.

My head between her legs, my tongue buried in her pussy.

I apologised.

I said that I had fucked up because I panicked about something that I already knew.

She made me work for her smile that I adore.

And then she pushed me to my knees and lifted her skirt.

Natalie knows what she wants, and I'm so fucking thankful that she seems to have some sort of addiction to my tongue. I mean, what other woman would command me in this way? Fucking no one. There is no other woman for me.

Even if I do end up having my throat slit by her father, it will have been worth it. She's worth it.

"Jesse," she moans out as she starts to climb the peak to her orgasm. I suck her clit harder, spear my fingers deeper inside of her, and then I take everything she has got to give.

There is no better sound than her moaning at the mercy of my mouth, hands or dick.

I stand up, licking my lips and the last bit of her pleasure off of me.

"Damn, Jesse, you sure do know how to apologise in style," she says with a wicked smirk on her face.

"You bring out the feral animal inside of me, Natalie."

"As long as I am the only woman that brings it out of you."

"Always. There will never be anyone else. I'm in this for the long haul, baby."

"Me too," she says before I claim her mouth with mine and bite her bottom lip. Honestly, she drives me fucking crazy in every way possible.

"Listen," she says as she places her hands on my chest and pulls her mouth away from mine. "I just want to say that I get that this is going to be difficult to keep quiet, and I know that we have months of secrecy ahead, but it won't be forever. One day I will be able to hold your hand in public, we will be able to kiss on a park bench while the sun is setting, we'll be allowed to hold hands whilst walking on the beach during a vacation, and we'll be able to show everyone that we are for keeps."

I find her hand with mine and link my fingers with hers before bringing her hand to my mouth and kissing the back of it. "I know, but it doesn't mean that I don't want to rip the head off of another guy touching you."

"I get that too, but I don't want anyone else. I only want you." The sincerity in her eyes nearly has me dropping to my knees again. I've never looked into someone's eyes before and felt like I am looking into their soul.

I never believed in soulmates.

I never realised how powerful love could be.

But Natalie has shown me that both of those things exist.

A knock on my office door has us springing apart.

Fuck.

Natalie gives me a wink before sauntering over to the storage cupboard at the back of my office, shutting herself inside and out of sight.

I blow out a breath and run my hands through my hair as I make my way to the door.

My heart is pounding so fucking fast I'm sure it's going to fly out of chest.

"Professor?" A voice says from the other side, and I instantly want to lock myself in the cupboard with Natalie.

I open the door, my face hard, my eyes narrowed.

Motherfucking Drake.

I already know he's here to kiss my ass and hope that I don't report his behaviour yesterday to the head, but he's out of luck because I already reported it and his parents are being informed about how he likes to threaten women, even though they probably won't listen.

"What do you want, Drake?"

"Can I have a word?"

I really don't want this asshole in my office, so I continue to block the door and stop him from entering.

"Go ahead," I say, my arms crossed over my chest, my jaw set tight.

He looks up and down the corridor. "Can I not come in?"

"No."

He gulps and I start to feel impatient.

"Well... I, uh... I just wanted to apologise for what I said the other day to Natalie," he starts, looking sheepish.

I wait a few beats because I am pretty sure that this can't be the whole conversation.

I wait a few more.

Turns out that he has nothing else to say.

Give me strength.

"Is that it?" I ask, looking as bored as ever. I know that I should try and show some enthusiasm for this conversation, but I have none, and I don't care to bother.

"I don't know what else you want me to say." He shrugs his shoulders, and I know that he has been told to come and apologise by the head and probably by his parents who like to sweep his behaviour under the carpet.

"I'm not really the one that you should be apologising to, am I?" I say with one eyebrow raised. "Your apology should go to Natalie because she is the one that you threatened."

"If you say so," he says with a snort and I swear, if I weren't a teacher, I may be tempted to throttle this asshole regardless of him being fifteen years younger than me. God, I'm going all fucking caveman again.

"Was there anything else?" I ask, wanting this prick to get away from me.

"No, Professor."

"Go, your next lecture starts soon." Fucker is in my next class.

He walks away, his shoulders slumped from not getting the reaction he wanted from me.

I shouldn't let my personal feelings get in the way, but even if Natalie wasn't mine, I would still be pissed that he had been threatening towards her, or any woman for that matter. One thing I won't tolerate is disrespect. It's not hard to be a nice person.

I close my office door, walk over to the cupboard and open the door.

Natalie stands there with a smile on her face.

"You know, I quite like it when you're assertive," she says, sauntering her sexy ass towards me.

"Oh yeah?"

"Yeah," she says as she links her arms around the back on my neck and places a kiss on my lips.

"I'll remember that in future."

"You better," she says before walking around me and to the office door. "See you in class, Professor." She winks and then opens the door, walking through it and out of my sight, leaving me with the biggest fucking smile on my face.

CHAPTER SIXTEEN

Natalie

Friday night.

It's been a tough week at Uni with assignments coming out of my ass, and I am ready to let loose and enjoy myself.

Sophia and I are on the dance floor in Tulip, Def Leppard, "Pour Some Sugar on Me," is blasting out of the sound system, and we are dancing up a storm. We've been drinking tequila which makes me more brazen than usual—if there is such a thing because I am pretty fucking brazen at the best of times.

We rock out to the music and I exert my best fucking moves as the chorus kicks in. I move my hips in time to the beat, belting out the words, Sophia doing the same.

I'm dressed to kill in my short denim mini-skirt, black sparkly halter-neck top and sky-high heels. My hair is pulled back in a high ponytail and I made sure my make-up was dramatic, completing it with bright red lipstick.

You could say I wanted to stand out from the crowd, and by fuck do I stand out.

Sophia looks absolutely gorgeous in her hot pants and gold top, her gold heels sparkling with each step she takes. We always have a good time when we are out, but tonight feels different, like we have both been waiting to truly unleash the vixens that we appear to have become tonight.

I have no interest in grabbing a man's attention, I dress for me and me alone.

Tulip is packed tonight, bodies everywhere. The DJ is smashing his set, and it's still only ten p.m.

As we sing along to the words, I throw my hands in the air and dance like I have never danced before. I feel amazing, and there isn't anyone that could dampen my glow tonight.

"Hot damn, Natalie, you are on fire, girl," Sophia shouts to me as the song wraps up and kicks into another absolute banger. I just smile at her and continue to lose myself in the rhythm.

I have to say that the last couple of weeks have been a whirlwind, but the best kind of whirlwind. Jesse came into my heart like a goddamn tornado, and he's been tearing up everything I ever thought I knew about love from the off.

I've always wanted a love like my mum and dad's. They are my role-models. My dad absolutely worships the ground my mother walks on, even as she challenges him and vice versa. Sure, sometimes their banter creeps me the fuck out because it would any child, but I see how fierce their love is, and I truly believe that I have that with Jesse.

It only takes a moment for that spark to ignite, for that zing to work its way into your veins, your heart, your soul. He's my zing, and I am his.

Would I like him to be here with me tonight? Of course, and it kills me a little that we can't just be a normal couple and show the whole world that we are one, but our time will come. We won't always need to hide in the shadows.

"Oh for fuck's sake," I hear Sophia say, and I come to an abrupt stop.

"What's wrong?" I ask. She nods her head in the direction behind me and I turn around to see fucking Drake stood there, leaning against the bar, a bottle of beer in his hand and a shit-eating grin on his face. He sees me looking and tilts his head before bringing the bottle of beer to his mouth and taking a glug. He's got two of his followers with him, Devon and Leo. They act like his goddamn groupies, kissing his ass all the time and jumping when he tells them how high.

"How the hell did he get in here?" Sophia asks the exact question I was just thinking.

"I don't know, but I'm about to go and find out," I say as I grab her hand and pull her behind me. I make a beeline for Marshall's office, knowing that he will be in there because that is where he stays until about midnight, not coming out until the cut off time for last entries into the club. I don't bother knocking when I get there, I'm fucking family, I never knock.

"Oh shit," Marshall says as I storm in, Sophia behind me, to see that there is some chick in front of him, her head bobbing up and down on his dick as he sits on the leather sofa.

I fold my arms across my chest and tap my foot, giving him a filthy look. I feel Sophia shudder behind me, and I know it's because she's always had a thing for Marshall, so seeing him being sucked off by some girl he probably doesn't even know the name of has got to hurt. The girl in question doesn't even stop what she is doing until Marshall pulls her away from him, quickly concealing himself and giving her a heads up that they have company.

I don't say a word as he composes himself and gets rid of the girl, shutting the door behind her.

"What the fuck, Nat?" he says, turning on me with a look of disbelief.

"So, this is why you let scum into your club, because you're too busy getting your dick wet to bother watching the fucking cameras?" I say, all shades of pissed off.

"And hello to you too," he says sarcastically. "Sup, Sophia."

She just makes a 'pfft' noise, clearly unimpressed by him at this moment in time.

Marshall looks just like a younger version on my Uncle Miles. He's got the blond hair which falls down to his shoulders, the darkest-coloured eyes that I have ever seen—almost black in their appearance—and full lips. He's a year younger than me, which is pretty young to be running a club, but Aunt Meghan wanted to give him a challenge seeing as he seemed to be pissing his life away before running Tulip. I have to say that she made the right decision in letting him run the place. He brings in the crowds, has DJ's queuing up to play here and a never-ending VIP list. Business brain he may have, but when it comes to seeing what is right in front of him—and by that, I mean Sophia—he is utterly clueless.

"So, what's up, cuz?" he says to me as he walks back behind his desk and takes a seat.

"What's up is that fucking Drake McCoy is stood in your club, drinking a beer like he belongs here," I say as I slam my hands on the top of his desk in frustration.

"How the hell did he get in here?" he says as he starts scanning the security cameras.

"Well, I'm guessing that your new doorman didn't get the memo that we don't let trash in here whilst you were busy getting your dick sucked by some hussy," I reply, my anger not diminishing in any way whatsoever.

"Okay, okay, calm the fuck down, Natty," he says, calling me by the nickname that he gave me when we were younger.

"I will not calm down. You know that he has no place being here, Marsh, and Uncle Miles would kick your ass if he knew that he had slipped past on your watch," I say, jabbing my finger towards him like I'm telling off a fucking toddler.

"Yeah, I get it, no reminder needed," he says as he stands up and buttons his suit jacket. "I'll go and take care of it now."

Marshall may be young, but he works hard to make sure he has rippling muscles that show in the outline of his suit. Honestly, he could rival the fucking Hulk.

"And what are you gonna do? Cause a scene in the middle of the club? Not only would your dad have your guts for garters, but so would my dad. They don't like it when you cause a scene, Marshall," I warn him.

"So what do you want me to do? Call him to one side and politely ask him to leave?" he says sarcastically.

"I know you have your stupid moments, Marshall, but now is not the time to have one of those."

"Fuck," he says as he stands there in silence for a beat. "You know, I'd love nothing more than to pop a fucking bullet in his head."

"Uh, guys, did you forget that I was in here?" Sophia says, and damn if I didn't do just that. She doesn't know the ins and outs of what our family do or have done. I tend to keep it quiet because it's none of anyone else's business. Plus, I don't want her to think differently of me. I know I don't usually give a shit about what others think, but Sophia is my best friend, and I wouldn't want to lose her friendship.

I turn to face her, and her eyes are a little wide.

"Marshall is just fucking around," I tell her, but I know that she doesn't believe that for one moment.

"Look, I'm not stupid, Nat. From some of the conversations we've had, I know that your family aren't exactly on the right side of the law, but did he really just talk about shooting someone without batting a fucking eyelid?" she says as she points at Marshall.

Uh oh. Time for damage control.

"It's complicated," I say. *Oh yeah, great damage control there, Natalie.*

"We've got time," she says, walking over to the chair in the corner and sitting herself down, crossing one leg over the other.

I look at Marshall and he gives me a nod, telling me that it will be okay and that we can trust her with our family's history.

"You have to promise me that you won't think any less of me," I start. "You're my best friend, and I hate that I haven't been able to be completely truthful with you, but there are reasons for it, and one of those reasons is that I don't want to lose your friendship, Sophia. I don't have many friends, only those I choose to let in." Which is pretty much just her at this point. Most other chicks get on my fucking nerves and I can't be doing with the dramatics that they bring with them.

"Do you think that I haven't heard the rumours about your family, Nat? I just chose not to ask you about them because I figured you would tell me when you were ready, but I gotta say, I'm not familiar with being around someone who openly says he wants to put a cap in someone's ass."

"Their head actually," Marshall says, and I elbow him in the side.

"We don't talk like that all the time," I say.

"I guess that I have to ask, are the rumours true?"

"Depends on what you have heard," Marshall says before I can respond.

"Let me see, what about the one where Joey and Paige

Valentine are known as legends in the underworld, is that one true?" she asks.

"Yes," I answer without hesitation, because I'm strangely proud that they ruled for so long.

"And what about the one where they were known to show their victims no mercy, even going as far as eradicating the Morgan brothers, three of the nastiest bastards to ever walk the earth?"

"True," I answer.

"I see," she says before pursing her lips.

"But they had reasons for doing those things, Sophia. My parents aren't evil."

"I never said they were," she says as she stands up. "In fact, your parents have been nothing but polite to me whenever I've been to yours, so who am I to judge them on their past without knowing all the facts?" She winks at me and I instantly feel like a weight has been lifted off of my shoulders.

"And it's actually pretty cool that my best friend has bad-as-fuck parents. I'll be sure to ask when I need someone putting in their place," she says and we both burst out laughing.

"You're not scared to still be friends with me?" I ask.

"Not at all. Actually, it's pretty much cemented the fact that you are never getting rid of me. I mean, Joey and Paige are fucking legends, and you will absolutely be telling me more at some point, but right now we gotta figure out a way of getting dickhead Drake out of here without a commotion."

"Christ, she learns the truth and five minutes later she's like one of the fucking crew?" Marshall says in disbelief.

"Pipe down, Marshy," she says, using the nickname that he hates with a passion. "We're about to get you out of a muddle and save your ass from getting kicked all over the place by your dad, and hers," she says as she slings her arm round my shoulders. "Come on, Nat, let's go." She walks us to the door and opens it, guiding us back to the main room.

"You got a plan in mind?" I ask her.

"Fuck no, but I bet you have."

"They don't call me a Valentine for nothing," I reply, feeling nothing but pride that I am indeed a motherfucking Valentine.

CHAPTER SEVENTEEN

Natalie

I DIDN'T EXPECT Sophia to take the news about my family as well as she did, but let's face it, she was bound to have heard about their history, most people have. Even Jesse knows for fuck's sake, although I don't know how much he knows because I've never asked the question.

I shake my head as I don't have time to think about Jesse right now. I hate to say it, but Drake is the only thing I am focussed on at this moment in time, and I wish to God that Marshall had kept his dick in his pants so that I wouldn't have to try and clean up his mess. It's not the first time I've had to help him, so to speak, but I don't think there will be any sweet-talking Drake, and to be honest, I wouldn't want to sweet-talk him.

Sophia and I make our way over to the parasite who is still stood at the bar with his goons.

"Ah, Natalie, Sophia," Drake says as we stop in front of him. "Can I get you a drink?"

"No thanks," Sophia says before I can speak.

"Then what can I do for you, ladies?"

"You can leave," I say, failing to hide my disgust for him.

"And why would I do that?" he asks, taking a swig of beer.

"Because you know damn well that you have no business being here," I say through gritted teeth. I try to keep my cool, but he just riles me with his cocky attitude and my-shit-doesn't-stink persona.

"And who's gonna make me leave? You?" he says, laughing, mocking me.

I'm not one for violence usually, but as I step forward, I grab his dick with my hand and squeeze. He drops his beer bottle to the floor where it smashes, and the remaining contents spill out. The music is loud enough in here that no one bats an eyelid. It also helps that he is stood in the corner, away from prying eyes.

"Don't make me rip it off, Drake," I say.

"If you wanted to touch my cock, Natalie, all you had to do was ask," he goads, and I twist my hand whilst tightening my hold. His eyes water and his face scrunches up from the pain. Good. Fucking asshole.

"You're lucky it's me stood here and not Marshall, Drake, because he wouldn't be letting you off this lightly. Now, I'll let go if you promise to walk out of here quietly and remember your place in future."

I stare him down, my resolve not weakening in the slightest. I tighten my hold again and a high-pitched squeal leaves him.

"Okay, okay, I'll go," he says, and I let go of him, making plans to disinfect my hand as soon as possible.

"Take your goons with you," I say with my head held high. Devon and Leo look petrified and like they want to run out of here with their tails between their legs. I resist the urge to laugh, I'll save that for when Sophia and I can continue our night that was supposed to be stress-free.

"That hate that you think you hold for me, Natalie, that's just the fire inside of you burning for me. I promise you that one day I'll have my dick buried so far inside of you that you'll be ruined for any other guy."

"In your dreams, Drake."

He smirks and signals to the other two to follow him. I can't help but snigger at the way he limps towards the exit.

"Jesus, Nat," Sophia says. "I knew that the Valentines were ruthless, but damn, you took charge like a badass."

"You've never seen my mother when she means business," I reply with a smile.

"I don't think I want to either," Sophia says.

"Drink?"

"Fuck yeah, I need it after that."

I laugh and we make our way to the VIP area, taking a seat at our usual table. In VIP we get table service, and the waitress comes straight over as soon as we have sat down and takes our drinks order.

Once she has wandered back to the bar, Marshall slides in the booth next to me.

"Fucking hell, Natty, what was that?" he asks, his eyes wide.

"What was what?"

"Don't piss about. You know damn well I mean what was that with you grabbing Drake's dick?" he says, and I struggle to contain my amusement.

"Well, it was either I grab his dick and cause him pain that way, or you cause a big commotion and have your ass handed to you," I say with a shrug of my shoulders.

"You know, if your dad finds out you did that then I'm dead anyway," he comments.

"Nah, he'll just make you suffer for a little bit, he wouldn't kill you, you're family."

"Gee, thanks for the reassuring words there, Natty," he says with an eyeroll.

"Look, Drake needed getting rid of, mission accomplished," I say as the waitress brings our drinks over and places them on the table. Marshall orders himself a soda and lime seeing as he doesn't drink any alcohol when he's working.

I wait for the waitress to return with his drink before raising my glass.

"To the next generation," I say to him and he lifts his glass, clinking it against mine.

"To the next generation. May the world prepare themselves for the next fucking level," he says before taking a sip of his drink.

"Next level,' I say with a wink, and even though I have no intention of becoming the next queen of the underworld, it sure is nice to know that I hold some sort of power already, and that I can roll with the best of them.

CHAPTER EIGHTEEN

Natalie

It's the punch to my jaw that knocks me off my balance.

A punch that came out of nowhere.

I was unprepared and still a little drunk from a night of consuming alcohol.

I'm still unprepared for the hands that push me against the wall, and for the fingers that grip my jaw, hard.

My eyes are a little blurry from the blinding pain of the punch and from the back of my head connecting with the wall. I furiously blink, trying to keep the tears from falling.

The one thing I need to do is not panic.

Easier said than done, but when you panic, you lose all control.

"You need to be taught a fucking lesson," the voice sneers at me, their lips by my ear. I recognise the voice instantly. Drake fucking McCoy.

I feel something trickle from my bottom lip and I run my

tongue along it, the metallic taste coating my mouth. He drew fucking blood.

"And why is that?" I say as I feel my control of my senses returning.

"You think you can just grab my dick and run me out of a club that we both know I belong in?"

A laugh escapes me at his words. "You don't belong here, and you won't belong anywhere when you're dead."

"Oooo, tough talk from the female pinned against the wall," he says sarcastically. "You think your big bad daddy is going to come after me? Get a grip, Natalie. I have power and status. My parents will shut down whatever shit your mob try to pull."

And there he goes, banking on the money and status to save him from the repercussions of this attack. What an utter fucking fool.

"I don't need anyone to save me, asshole. I can take care of myself," I grit out.

"Again, I'll remind you of who is pinning who against this wall."

"Only because you came at me like the coward that you are and took me by surprise."

"Oh, baby," he says as he runs his thumb down my cheek and across my bottom lip, blood covering his thumb. He licks my blood off of his thumb and then moves closer to my face and runs his tongue across my lip. "Mmm, tastes good." His smile is evil, and I swear to God that he will not get away with this. It takes all of my willpower not to flinch away from him and show him that I am affected by his behaviour.

"One day soon, this won't just be blood that I'll be tasting, it'll be your pussy when I make you come so hard that it's dripping down your legs."

"In your fucking dreams, Drake."

"You have no idea," he says.

Ugh. He repulses me, and if he ever tries to come near me with his dick, I'll cut the damn thing off.

"And I'll tell you something else... I'll fuck you a damn sight better than that Professor you're currently opening your legs for."

His words shock the hell out of me.

What. The. Hell?

He knows?

How the fuck does he know?

We've been so careful... haven't we?

"Yeah, that's right, I've seen you. You think you've been sly about it? Pah, couldn't have been more fucking obvious if you tried. I've watched, I've waited, and now you'll be at my fucking mercy. So, here's the deal. I'll keep my mouth shut about the Professor sticking his dick in you, as long as you keep this little chat between the two of us quiet. Is that clear?" he says with a smug fucking look on his face.

I grind my teeth together, and I have no doubt that if I had a gun in my hand right now, I would shoot this asshole and rid the world of one more parasite. I've never had the urge to kill anyone before, but I'd make an exception for him.

"Crystal," I say.

He moves his face towards me, roughly turns my head to the side and runs his tongue up the side of my face. "And if you're lucky then I'll bring my knife out to play—"

"Natalie?"

I hear my name being shouted by Sophia and I pray that she walks around the corner of the club and sees me.

Drake momentarily pauses, his grip on my face loosening slightly. "Guess our time is up for now, but I just have one last parting gift for you..." His voice trails off and before I can register anything, he's punched me in the stomach, leaving me gasping for breath. "Until next time, sweetheart." And then he's gone as I struggle to breathe through the pain.

I can still hear Sophia calling my name as I try to breathe slowly, allowing the nausea to wash over me.

I close my eyes, Drake's words replaying on a loop in my mind.

"I'll fuck you a damn sight better than that Professor."

"I'll bring my knife out to play."

I use every ounce of strength left in me to move my feet. It takes me a minute to round the corner of the club, but when I do, Sophia comes running over to me, her eyes wide.

"Oh my God, Natalie," she says, taking in my hunched posture and my cut lip. "What the hell happened?" She moves to the side of me and puts her arm around me, helping me stay upright.

"I…" What do I say? Do I tell her that Drake did this?

"Natalie." She says my name desperately and I can see that she is frantic to know what happened. "Your lip—"

"I know, I probably look hideous," I say, trying to crack a joke but failing miserably. I can feel tiredness seeping over me from a night of drinking alcohol, dancing, and getting beat.

"We need to get you home," she says, but that is the last place I want to go right now.

"No… I… I need to go to Jesse."

"Jesse? Who the fuck is Jesse?" she asks, looking confused.

I take a deep breath as I see our taxi pull up to the curb, and I know that this is going to bring with it a whole load of questions that I'm not sure I'm ready to answer but might have to anyway.

"Professor Marks. Jesse," I say breathlessly as we walk to the taxi, the pain still ricocheting through me, making me want to curl into a ball and pass out.

Sophia opens the taxi door and I gently get in, the throbbing in my stomach seeming to get worse with every movement. I rattle off Jesse's address to the driver, and once Sophia has slid in beside me, we're off. It won't take long to get there, about ten minutes. I just need him. I don't want to speak to anyone else until I have spoken to him.

"Natalie, why the fuck are we going to Professor Mark's house?" Sophia whispers so the driver can't hear what we are saying.

"I'll explain everything when we get there, but right now, I just need to see him." I'm aware that my voice sounds a little slurred, but my energy is dwindling rapidly along with my adrenaline.

"Are you..." Her voice trails off.

"Not now, Sophia."

A few seconds pass between us, and all the time I can feel her eyes on me, assessing me.

"Oh my God, you are, aren't you?" If I thought she looked shocked earlier, then that's nothing to how she looks now.

I nod my head and turn to look out of the window. This is not how I was hoping she would find out. I wanted to be able to tell her when the time was right, but now Drake has pushed me into revealing my secret a lot sooner than I would have liked.

I have no idea how things are going to go when we get to his house.

I have no idea what I am going to do to stop Drake from thinking he has some sort of hold over me.

And I have no idea how I am going to stop my parents from losing their absolute shit about all of this.

I feel my eyes getting heavy as we drive along, and I close them, trying to calm my raging thoughts.

CHAPTER NINETEEN

Jesse

THERE'S A KNOCKING at my front door. I check the time to see that it is nearly four in the morning. I have no idea who the hell would be trying to break down my front door at this time of night, because that's what it sounds like as I pull on a T-shirt and my grey joggers that I left on the floor when I crawled into bed.

I make my way down the stairs, the banging echoing through the house.

"Alright, I'm coming," I shout as I reach the bottom step and head to the front door.

Unlocking it, I am ready to give whoever it is a piece of my mind, until I see that it's Sophia from one of my classes, and Natalie.

Oh my fucking God... Natalie.

There is blood smeared down her chin, Sophia has her arm around her like she is propping her up, and she's holding her stomach.

"Jesus," I say as I step forwards and replace Sophia's arm with my own. I don't even think as I put my other arm behind her legs and pick her up, cradling her in my arms as I take her inside. I don't register anything else as I carry her into the lounge, flicking the light switch on before carrying her over to the sofa. I gently lie her down and kneel beside her, pushing the loose hair that has escaped from her ponytail out of her face.

"What the hell happened?" I ask as I take in her pale face and her cut lip.

"She was attacked after we left Tulip," Sophia says from behind me, and it is at this point that I turn around and register her stood there. Another student in my house, I'd get fucking prosecuted if anyone found out, and I don't fucking care. All I care about is finding out who put their hands on Natalie.

"By who?" I ask.

"I don't know, she hasn't told me."

I turn my attention back to Natalie. "Baby, who did this?"

She looks tired, but I need to know. I don't care that I've called her baby in front of Sophia, if she wants to report me then she can go right ahead. I always knew the risks going into this relationship, and Natalie means too much to me to just throw away what we have.

"Jesse, we have a problem," she whispers.

"Damn right we have a problem, one that I want to go and take care of right fucking now."

"You can't," she says, her eyes struggling to stay open.

"Of course I can, I just need to know who did this," I tell her. She can't expect me to do nothing.

"No, you have to let this go."

"No fucking chance, Natalie." Is she crazy? How on earth am I going to be able to let this shit go? "Just tell me who did this to you."

"Not until you promise not to do anything stupid."

I can't promise her that.

I keep my mouth closed; my teeth clenched together.

"Come on, Natalie," Sophia says. "We need to know."

Natalie looks at Sophia before returning her gaze to me. She looks worried, fearful, and a dread seeps its way into my stomach.

"He knows about us," she whispers, so fucking quiet that I think I misheard her. But I didn't. Someone knows about us, that very same someone that attacked her tonight.

"Who?" I say, my voice low, my eyes trained on hers.

"Drake."

"Motherfucker," I say as I stand up, my hands balled into fists at my sides.

"Drake did this?" Sophia says, moving to kneel in the place that I just vacated. Natalie nods and the blood heats inside of me.

Fucking Drake McCoy.

"I guess he was pissed that we made him leave Tulip, and then he told me that he knows about me and Jesse," Natalie says to Sophia. She bites her bottom lip and then winces.

"Christ," I mutter as I start to pace the length of the room. "Why did you make him leave Tulip?"

"Because he's not welcome there," Sophia answers.

"Can I get some water, please?" Natalie says and I feel like an absolute asshole for not getting her a drink sooner.

"Of course," I say as I leave the room and go to the kitchen. I take a glass out of the cupboard and fill it with tap water. I'm so consumed by my thoughts that I almost drop the glass when I hear Sophia speak from behind me.

"I'm not going to say anything."

I turn around and lean against the worktop. "We didn't plan on this happening."

"You don't have to explain yourself to me," she says.

"I know that, I'm just saying that we couldn't control what happened between us." I feel like I need Sophia on my side because she is Natalie's best friend, and we need someone to approve of us.

"Let me take her the water whilst you take a minute to get yourself together," Sophia says as she walks over and holds her hand out for the glass. I pass it to her, and she nods her head at me before turning and walking to the kitchen door.

She pauses and looks back around at me. "Do you care for her?"

"I love her," I say without missing a beat.

She smiles and then disappears, taking Natalie her drink.

I need to do something, anything to stop myself from picturing Drake with his hands on her, hurting her, making her bleed.

The problem with being older is that it will look ten times worse if I go after him, not to mention that I am the bastard's Professor.

For once in my life, I truly wish that I hadn't become a teacher. But then I may never have met Natalie, so I need to stop thinking that way.

I tap my foot as I think of my next move.

But I already know what I have to do.

I walk back into the lounge to see Natalie sat up, drinking her water, Sophia sat beside her. I kneel in front of Natalie, placing my hands on her knees.

"Natalie, you know that things can't be left this way. Drake doesn't get to run the show here," I tell her, and she nods her head at me. I take a deep breath before saying my next words. "And that is why we need your parent's here."

Natalie's eyes go wide, as do Sophia's.

"Are you crazy?" Sophia asks me. "You know who her parents are, don't you?"

"Yes."

"They will kill you," Sophia continues.

"And that's a risk I'm willing to take," I say sincerely. Anything to keep Natalie safe. "Give me your phone, baby."

Natalie looks at me with so much love in her eyes that I feel it penetrate right to my heart.

"I know why you're saying this, and I know why you're thinking that this is the only option, but it isn't," she says, her eyes fluttering closed before slowly opening again.

"Of course it's the only option. Fuck, Natalie, they need to know," I say, exasperation lacing my tone.

"Not yet they don't."

"Nat, come on, your parents aren't going to let this slide, you know that they are going to want to know who did this to you," Sophia says.

"If they find out about Drake attacking me, they are going to want to know why, and they can't know that... Not yet," Natalie says, and I go to her, kneeling down, taking her hand in mine.

"I love that you want to protect what we have, but now is not the time, Natalie. We have to stop Drake from doing anything else, he can't be allowed to run the show," I say, my eyes boring into her's as I try to make her see sense.

She shakes her head a little, then hisses as her movements clearly cause some sort of pain.

"You're not thinking straight, you need to let me handle this—"

"Like fuck do I," I interrupt. "You are not going anywhere near that asshole."

"Stop," she says, squeezing my hand gently. "Drake isn't going to say anything. He's going to think that he is in control here, but really, he's just the fucking puppet to our strings."

"Nat, you're not making any sense," Sophia says.

"Maybe not to you, but once the shock and anger wears off, you'll see that my way is the best way."

"And what the hell are you going to tell your parents?" Sophia asks, the shock apparent in her tone.

"Wrong place, wrong time, and that I have no idea who did this."

"You're playing with fire, Natalie, and you know it," Sophia argues.

"Well, it's a good job that I have Valentine blood running through me then, isn't it?" she sasses, and damn if she doesn't make my fucking heart sing. Here she is, busted lip, bruises God knows where else because I haven't even asked that question yet, and still, she has a plan formulating. Must be in the fucking genes because I'm pretty sure that her parents weren't the leaders of the underworld for nothing.

I can see that Natalie needs to rest, so I opt for the easiest choice at this moment in time. "I think we all need to get some sleep, take some time and figure this out in the morning," I say, even though I already know that I won't be sleeping because all I will be picturing is that motherfucker hitting her, touching her, putting his goddamn hands on her. My blood boils beneath the surface, but I'm trying to keep it locked up, for Natalie's sake. If she can be level-headed about this, then I sure as shit need to try and do the same thing.

I stand up and then crouch down, placing one arm under Natalie's legs and the other around the bottom of her back as I lift her into my arms effortlessly.

"You need sleep," I say before turning to Sophia. "I have spare pillows and a blanket upstairs if you want to sleep on the sofa." I can't turf her out at this time of night, or morning rather.

"Uh..." Sophia looks uncomfortable, and to be honest, I feel awkward about this too, but there is no way I am letting her make her way home at this ridiculous hour on her own, even if my ass is on the line here.

"You can leave as soon as its light if that makes you feel

better," I offer with a forced smile. This is weird as fuck, but she brought Natalie to me, she's her friend, and ultimately, she's on our side... I think.

"Thanks, Professor."

"Oh God, please, just call me Jesse," I say. It's awkward enough without her addressing me so formally.

"Okay, Jesse... Wow, that sounds so weird," she says with a laugh.

"I'll be back in a sec with the blanket and pillows," I say before striding from the room, Natalie curled against me, her hand resting on my chest, her face nuzzled in the crook of my neck. I walk from the lounge to the stairs and am soon entering my bedroom, placing her gently on the bed. She lets out a little groan.

"Where does it hurt?" I ask her.

"My stomach," she says with a wince.

"Show me."

"It's nothing."

"Natalie." I say her name with warning lacing my tone.

She sighs and moves her hands away from her stomach. I gently move her top up and am fucking appalled to see that she has a bruise the size of a fist forming on her beautiful skin. I can feel the rage burning inside of me like an inferno.

Who the fuck does Drake think he is?

What gives him the right to put his hands on any woman?

I take a few deep breaths, trying to calm the fuck down.

Natalie raises her hand and cups the side of my face. "I'm okay, Jesse." The smile she gives me almost breaks my fucking soul. She is inside of me, buried deep, and she makes me feel every-fucking-thing.

I close my eyes briefly, dropping my head, shaking it from side to side.

"You don't need to act so brave all the time, you know," I tell her, bringing my eyes to hers, letting her see all of me.

Our relationship has shifted significantly, and my love for her runs through my veins. I will never be able to let her go. She's mine, regardless of our goddamn ages or how we met. I've never experienced this level of ferocity before. I would fight for her, I would die for her, I would fuck shit up for her. I think it's safe to say that any morals I still had have flown out of the window, along with any rational thought.

She's changed me.

She's unmasked me.

She's made me see that there is more to life than teaching.

Before her, I didn't really have much. Work and home, saw my friends occasionally, spent weekends doing not a fucking lot.

And now? Now I have her to live for, to breathe for.

"He won't get away with this," she says, breaking me from my thoughts.

"No, he won't, and I sure as shit want to be there when he has his ass handed to him," I say with confidence. Fuck the hiding, I'm ready to ride the storm that will come from our secret being made public knowledge.

"You know as well as I do that you can't be there when Drake gets his just desserts."

"Like fuck I can't!" I exclaim.

"Jesse, you can't be anywhere near this. You have a career—"

"That I no longer fucking want," I say, cutting her off.

She sighs. "You don't mean that. You're just angry right now."

"I'll be angry until the day I die about the fact that Drake put his fucking hands on you," I growl.

She smirks. "You going rogue on me, Jesse?"

"Damn straight."

"Quite the turnaround, huh, Professor?" she teases.

"When it comes to you, Natalie, there are no fucking rules."

"Rules were made to be broken," she whispers, her eyes holding mine.

"It seems so," I say with a nod of my head.

"You ready to trade in everything you think you know just to be a part of my world?" she asks, and I see the nerves that she tries to hide at asking that question.

"In a heartbeat."

"You're my ride or die, Jesse."

"And you're mine too."

CHAPTER TWENTY

Natalie

It appears that my pussy has powers that I never knew existed.

Somewhere along the line, Jesse went from being my hot as fuck Professor to being my hot as fuck boyfriend, who has apparently decided to trade in his soul just to be with me and to be a part of my sinister world.

My parents have always tried to shield me from the dark and shady shit that they have dealt with for years, but sometimes, the shield needs to be broken.

I can't rely on everyone else to deal with my problems, and I certainly don't want to put Jesse's whole fucking life on the line just so he can help me deal with Drake McCoy.

No.

I need to figure this shit out, and quick.

I have no doubt that Jesse wants to move heaven and earth for me, but I am a Valentine and I have the blood of my mother and father running through me. Relying on others isn't even a fucking option, and I'll be damned if I am going to put Jesse in harm's way. Because that is what would happen here. He wouldn't have the first clue about how my world works. I've been born into it, heard the stories, witnessed a couple of stand-offs whilst hiding in the wings, and I know that I can deal with whatever comes my way.

It's why I decided to train in criminal law.

I wanted to know how it worked on the other side because then I have the power to save the asses of those who go to fucking bat for me and for my family.

I need to have that power so that I can laugh all the way to the fucking court, knowing that I can take down those who decide to target the Valentine empire.

I push the doors of Tulip open and storm my way to Marshall's office.

You see, he's the one that I go to when I need a little help handling shit. You always have that one family member that has no cut off point, doesn't know when to quit, will keep going until there is no other outcome other than death... Marshall is that for me. He's a crazy motherfucker when he wants to be, and together we will eventually take over and run the family business.

My parents want me to have no part of it, and up until recently, I had no intention of trying to rule the underworld, but shit changes and now I want it all. They have always wanted me away from the danger, away from the assholes that hide in the dark, but I want this life. I want to be respected, feared, loved. My mum and dad have been all three in their lifetime, and so have Marshall's parents. They've all worn the crown, and now it's our turn. We just have to make sure that we prove ourselves first, and I'm going to start with Drake fucking McCoy.

I kick the door open to Marshall's office, letting it bang against the wall.

"Do come in," Marshall says, not even looking up from the paperwork on his desk.

"We have a problem," I tell him, and only then does he look up and get his first glimpse of my face.

"What the fuck happened to you?" he says as he drops the pen he was writing with and gets up from the chair, rounding the desk and coming to stand in front of me.

"Oh, you know, a little slap and tickle."

"Don't fuck around, Natalie," he scolds me.

I roll my eyes. "When I left here last night, I got jumped, took a couple of punches."

"Who did this?" he asks, his jaw clenched.

Now that's the million-dollar question, and I still don't know if I am going to tell him the truth or not.

"Let's just say that I had a run in with an asshole, and I need to take the fucker down."

"Said in true Valentine style," he remarks with a smirk. "But seriously, who hit you, Natty?"

"I can't tell you that until you promise me that what I say in here goes no further."

"In other words, don't tell your mum and dad?" he questions, hitting the nail on the head. I don't say anything as he watches me for a few seconds before taking a step back and running his hands through his hair. "Jesus, Natty, you know that Uncle Joey and Aunt Paige will have my ass if they ask me what I know and I don't tell them."

"You wanna be next level with me, Marshall?" I ask him, knowing that he wants the crown as much as I do.

"You know that I do, I've been planning this shit for the last couple of years."

"Then I need to know that I can trust you—"

"You have always been able to trust me," he says, cutting me off and looking at me like I've just said the most ridiculous thing.

"This is different," I start. "If I tell you what this is all about then I need to know that the threat of my dad cutting your dick off isn't going make you talk."

A few moments of silence, the tick-tock of the clock seeming to echo around the room.

"Total trust?" he asks, saying the words that we've heard our parents say to each other a few times.

"Total trust," I reply with a nod.

"Fuck, Natalie... You know I've always got your back, so hit me with it."

"The person that attacked me was Drake McCoy," I begin. "He caught me off-guard outside of here, took me round the side of the club, made threats, got a couple of punches in."

"What's he got on you?" Marshall asks.

"He knows that I've been sleeping with my Professor from Uni—"

"What the fuck, Natty?" Marshall says, his voice loud.

"Let me finish before you judge, Marshall." I wait a beat to make sure he pipes the fuck down before I continue. He moves back behind his desk and takes a seat, leaning back, and I take that as my cue to continue. "Drake threatened me with exposing my relationship, and before you ask, it's not just about sex."

"I wasn't actually going to ask that," Marshall says, giving me a "what the fuck" look.

I can't help the chuckle that leaves me. "I love him, Marshall, and he loves me. Drake wants to fuck with me, with us probably, and he's going to use this to his advantage. He can't have an advantage. He needs to fucking disappear."

"You know as well as I do that he can't just disappear, Natalie."

I know this, but it doesn't mean that I like it.

"So, I need to shut him up another way... And I think I have an idea," I continue.

"Well then, I'm all ears," Marshall says as he puts his feet up on the desk, hands behind his head, looking every inch the hungry asshole that wants to go and start shit.

I move forward and take the seat on the other side of Marshall's desk, giving the sofa a wide berth seeing as he was getting his dick sucked on there last night.

"Just answer me one thing before we go any further," he says, moving his legs back off the desk and bracing his elbows on the desk, leaning forwards a little. "This Professor... Is he your ride or die?"

"Yes." I don't even hesitate in my answer.

"Are you his?"

"Yes."

He nods his head a few times before letting a smirk grace his face. "Well then, Natty, you better tell me what the plan is, and make sure it contains an element of me having some fun."

I smile back at him. His type of fun involves knives, screwdrivers and a cut-throat razor.

"Oh, you'll get to have your fun, Marshall, no doubt about it."

CHAPTER TWENTY-ONE

Jesse

"Brody, I need a favour."

I never ever thought that I would make a phone call like this, but life throws curveballs at you and you just have to make sure you swerve them as best as you can, or hit them head-on, just like I am right now.

"Sure, what's up, dude?" Brody says down the phone.

"I need you to get me a free pass to meet with Joey Valentine."

"Uh...W... Why?" Brody stutters.

"Because."

"I'm gonna need a better reason than that, dude."

"I can't give you a better reason, Brody, I just need a meeting with him," I say with my teeth gritted together in frustration.

"Jesse, there is no way on this fucked-up earth that I can get you a meeting without a good fucking reason," Brody replies, and I start to feel my patience wear thin.

"You know that I wouldn't be asking if it wasn't important."

"Yeah, I might know that, but Joey certainly won't. I can't just rock up to him and ask him to meet with someone he doesn't fucking know and has no reason to meet with."

"Fuck's sake," I say as I clench my hand into a fist.

"What's going on, Jesse? Why the sudden interest in Joey Valentine?" Brody asks me.

"I just..." I just what? I need to speak with him because I'm fucking his daughter... no, I'm in love with his daughter... either response is going to end with my dick being blown off. "Can you get me an in for Club Valentine?" I try a different approach.

"Are you part of the underworld?"

"No."

"Do you have connections to the underworld?"

"I'm friends with you," I say.

"Not gonna cut it, Jesse."

Bollocks.

"I need this, Brody."

"I can tell, but I'm still going to need to know why," he replies.

"Is it that you need to know, or that you don't actually have the sway to get me in there?" I say, knowing this will push his buttons.

"The fuck did you say?"

"You heard me, Brody. You always say that you're a top runner, they couldn't do without you, they trust you, need you, you bring in the most money... So, put that money where your mouth is and get me a goddamn meeting with him." I'm being an ass, I'm fully aware of that fact, but I need this. I need to be a fucking man and face my problems, even if that means I have to jump headfirst into the lion's den.

"Jesse, are you on crack or something? What is going on?"

Brody asks, trying again to get me to talk. "I've known you a long fucking time, and never once have you asked to come into my world."

"I know... I'm... I'm desperate, Brody, and trust me when I tell you that you want no part of what I need to do."

"If I get you a meeting with him then I'm already a fucking part of it, that's how it works," Brody tells me, and I feel like I'm fighting a losing battle here. "I want to help you, man, I really do, but you have no idea who you're fucking with here."

Oh, I do.

I have every idea of who I'm fucking with... and she's totally worth it.

I want to be the man that she deserves, and if that means going toe-to-toe with her father, then so be it.

"Are you in trouble?" Brody asks me.

"You have no idea."

"Shit, man, and you need Joey to help you out?"

"In a way, yes."

"But he's not even the one in charge anymore, so why would he be the one you go to?"

I was hoping that he wouldn't ask me that question, but he has, and I have no response for him.

"You know what? It doesn't matter, I'm just being stupid." I roll my eyes at my pathetic excuse for wanting to meet with one of the most notorious leaders ever to have lived.

"When you finally want to tell me the truth, Jesse, then give me a call, but until then, I can't help you," Brody says.

"I get that," I say with a snort. After everything I've done for him, he can't even do this for me.

"I'm sorry, man."

"Yeah, me too."

"Gotta say though, I'm a little more than intrigued to know what the hell is going on with you right now."

"Hmm," I mumble. I'm not telling him shit, because although he may have been my friend for a long time, he's still a drug runner, and his loyalties have clearly shifted. There would have been a time that he would have done this for me, but not now. "Listen, Brody, can we keep this between us? Forget this conversation ever happened?"

"Already forgotten, dude."

I mumble my thanks and end the call.

It seems like I'll just have to think of another way to get that meeting with Joey.

CHAPTER TWENTY-TWO

Natalie

I TAKE a deep breath and push the door open. I have avoided coming home all morning, but it's time to face my parents. They are going to fucking freak.

I close the front door, and no sooner have I taken another step, my mother is coming out of the kitchen, the smile quickly dropping from her face when she sees me.

"Natalie," she says as she rushes towards me, cupping my face in her hands. "What the hell happened to you?"

"What, no hello first?" I say, trying to keep things light, but I should have known that there would be no light to be shed on this moment.

"Natalie Valentine, who did this to you?" Mum says, her face rigid.

"Jeez, Mum, can't I get a cup of coffee first?" I say as I move out of her hold and walk around her, heading for the kitchen.

I feel her following me as I enter the kitchen, breathing a

sigh of relief that my dad isn't in here. I know that it is a matter of minutes before he finds out that I came home with a busted face, but I'll take those few minutes to try and get myself together for his interrogation.

I busy myself getting a mug out of the cupboard before my mum's voice stops me in my tracks. "You have about two seconds to sit your ass down, young lady." The way she says it has me placing the mug down—minus the coffee—and making my way over to one of the stools that are placed around the kitchen island. She takes a seat opposite me and I prepare myself to tell her a bare-faced lie.

"Firstly, are you okay?" she asks, concern etched on her face.

"I'm fine, Mum."

She nods her head slowly. "Secondly, what happened?"

I take a deep breath. "I got jumped outside Tulip when I was leaving last night."

"This happened last night? And you didn't think to come home sooner?"

"I went back to Sophia's as planned." Lie.

"Why not come home?"

"Because I didn't want to worry you at three in the morning when there was nothing that could have been done," I say with a shrug of my shoulders.

"Now, I know you don't believe the bullshit that just came out of your mouth," she scolds. "Try again, baby girl, and make me believe you this time."

Shit.

Oh God.

Okay, I can do this.

"I didn't want you or Dad to do anything reckless because of me," I say. I genuinely wouldn't want them to do anything reckless, so this isn't a total lie.

She takes a moment, letting my words sink in, eyeing me from across the island.

"How many were there?" she asks, seeming to move on from her previous question.

"One."

"Who?"

"I don't know." I hold her gaze, poker face in place.

The seconds tick by, but I don't falter. If I falter now, then she will definitely know that I am lying.

Tick, tick, tick.

"Woman or man?" is her next question.

"A man."

"Old? Young?"

"I'm not sure. After they punched me in the face, my vision blurred, and I couldn't get a clear look at them."

"Where was Sophia?"

"Inside Tulip, using the toilet. I said that I would go and wait outside for the taxi, and that's when it happened." Fuck, my nerves feel like they are all over the damn place, but I have the determination of both of my parents, and I know that I can mask it just as well as they can.

"You been to see Marshall?"

"Yes, that's why I didn't come straight home this morning. I figured the CCTV may have caught something, but it didn't," I tell her.

"Hmm." It's the only response she gives before my dad walks into the room.

"Good morning, lad—" He stops talking as he looks at my face. "What the fuck happened?" he growls as he walks over to me, surveying my injuries, much like my mum did when she first saw me.

"Mum can tell you, I really just need to go and lie down," I say, feeling exhausted all of a sudden.

"I don't think so, I want to know what the hell happened,

and I want to know right fucking now," he says, his voice low and dangerous.

I really don't want to do this again. I don't want to keep lying. I hate it. But I know it is the only way to protect Jesse, and I would protect him time and time again.

"Dad, please—"

"No, Natalie," he says, cutting me off. "I walk in here to see your lip split, a fucking bruise surrounding it, and you just want to go and have a lie down?"

"Joey," my mum says, a clear warning in that one word alone.

"No," he turns to look at her, his eyes blazing. "Don't do that, Paige."

His warning seems to fall on deaf ears as my mum dismisses me. "Go, get some rest, we'll talk later." She may be talking to me, but her eyes never leave my dad's. It's like they are in some silent stand-off, and I for one am happy to get the fuck out of here.

I silently make my way from the room, the tension feeling thicker with every step taken.

I walk along the hallway and up the stairs, the silence deafening.

I know that my parents are about to have crossed words, but I'm too tired to care right now.

Mentally exhausted.

Physically bruised.

And feeling like the shittiest daughter ever for lying to them.

I don't even get undressed as I crawl onto my bed and slide under the duvet, letting tears of frustration fall.

I must have been asleep for hours because when I open my eyes the room is dark. I reach over and click my bedside lamp on, only to squint from the sudden burst of light.

It takes a few seconds for my eyes to focus.

I slowly sit up, wincing from the pain that seems to ricochet through my body as I slump against the headboard. Damn, Drake really did a fucking number on me. My body aches and my lip stings. I bring my hand up to the cut that is going to look fucking spectacular for the next few days and run my hand over it, hissing from the pain as I do so.

I take a few deep breaths and then realise that I need to move my ass and figure out exactly how I am going to put my plan in motion. Get Drake on his own, lure him in and then video the fucker confessing to his sins and begging for his life. It will be enough, and I will use myself as the goddamn bait, because I want to see this asshole squirm, and I want to be the one to make him do it. He's always had an obsession with my pussy, and he's going to wish that he hadn't.

Marshall didn't seem struck on my plan at first, but when I told him that he would be there, waiting in the wings, ready to doll out a little bit of brutality, he was more than up for the challenge. I would never allow myself to be in a room on my own with Drake, but he doesn't know that, and now I have to make sure I build things up correctly. I can't just walk up to Drake and make out I want to suck his dick after everything that has happened, it would be obvious that I was up to something, and I need Drake to stay in the goddamn dark.

I also need to speak to Jesse and make sure that he doesn't do anything stupid. I know that he is a full-grown man who can control his own mind, but fuck, the look in his eyes at the thought of Drake hurting me. The way in which he looked at me, said he wanted to be a part of my world and that I was his ride or die... Biggest fucking turn on ever.

I'm not a girl that wants flowers and chocolates, I'm a

woman that wants a man to lay down his fucking life for me. And I have that with Jesse.

I gingerly move myself off of the bed and walk to my bedroom door, all the while keeping my ears pricked for any signs that my parents may be talking, but it's deadly quiet as I descend the stairs and make my way into the kitchen.

"Mum? Dad?" I call out as I walk to the lounge first, then the home gym before heading to their shared office space.

Empty. Every single room empty.

I don't know whether to be relieved or worried.

I know for a fact that they won't be taking a casual stroll around the block... No, they'll be trying to find out what the hell happened to me, and I pray to God that if they have gone to see Marshall that he doesn't spill the beans. This will be the biggest test of our relationship. If he spills, I'm out. I can't run an empire with someone that I can't trust implicitly.

With a sigh, I drag my weary body back to my bedroom and grab my phone from my bedside table. I quickly find Jesse's number and hit the call button. I just need to speak to him, to hear his voice, to know that he is okay.

After three rings he picks up, and I breathe a sigh of relief.

"Hey, baby," he says, and I smile.

"Hey, you."

"How are you feeling?" he asks.

"I'm okay, Jesse."

"Don't bullshit me, Nat," he says, and I can hear that dangerous tone lurking deep in his voice, and damn if it doesn't make my pussy tingle. Maybe he will fit into my world a lot easier than I thought?

"I'm a little sore, but nothing that a nice warm bath won't fix," I reply, a teasing edge to my voice.

"You getting in the bath now?"

I smirk and make my way to my ensuite. "Just running the

water," I say as I turn the hot tap on and pour in some bubbles before shutting the door and sliding the lock into place. "You know, it's a shame that I'm here all alone... naked." I quickly rid myself of my clothes and hear him suck in a breath.

"Fuck, Nat, you shouldn't be talking like that," he says, and I feel my face frown.

"Why not?"

"Because you've just been attacked and here I am, getting a fucking stiffy at the thought of you in the bath tub," he says, making me chuckle.

"A stiffy? Showing your age there, Professor," I tease.

"Fuck my age, you know that it doesn't mean anything when we're together."

"I know," I whisper, because age is nothing but a number, and I wouldn't change us for anything. "You know what else I know?"

"What's that?" he asks as I test the water before adding a bit of cold to it.

"I know that my phone has a great hands-free-speaker..." I let my voice drift off as I turn the cold tap off and switch the speaker on, placing the phone at the end of the bath before climbing in. I sigh as the hot water hits my skin. "And I know that my hands need occupying," I finish as I lie back and wait to see what he says.

"Jesus fucking Christ," he says, and I smile. "What are you doing to me, Natalie?"

"We're gonna have some fun after the shit-show of the last twenty-four hours. So, you got your cock in your hand, Jesse?" I ask, getting straight to the point. "Because I'm ready and waiting, my hands sliding down my body, resting at the top of my thighs."

"Keep going," he says.

"Keep going where?" I tease.

"Open your legs wide and move your hand so your fingers stroke up and down your lips." I do as he says and spread my legs as wide as the bath with allow, which is pretty fucking wide because I do not have a standard size bath. I start to stroke and let out a groan as my finger brushes against my clit with my movements.

"Move your other hand to your breast and pinch your nipple, close your eyes and imagine I'm there with you," he continues. "Imagine me kissing you, touching you, moving my thumb on your clit, pushing my fingers inside of you..."

"Jesse," I whisper as I feel my heart rate start to climb.

"Circle your clit, baby, slowly." I do and fuck if I don't need more. I need him.

"I need you, Jesse," I tell him.

"You have me, always, forever." His words push me a little bit higher and I move my hand from my breast and place it at my opening before pushing two fingers inside of me. I move them back and forth as I quicken my pace.

"Oh God," I say on a breath. "I'm gonna come."

"Wait for me, I'm nearly there," Jesse says, and I hear him groan which does nothing to stop my pleasure.

"Faster, Jesse, go faster, imagine my mouth wrapped around you, my tongue swirling at the tip, tasting you, wanting you to—"

"Fuck, now, Natalie, come for me," he says, and I stop holding back. I move my fingers in and out faster, circle my thumb quicker and apply a little more pressure, and then I'm exploding, my release coming quick and fast. I hear Jesse roar as we both climax, our combined moans seeming to echo all around me.

I listen to his breathing as I try to control mine.

"I wish I was with you," I say, never meaning anything more.

"Ditto, baby."

"One day soon, we won't have to hide."

"You got a plan, Natalie?"

"Don't I always?" I say with a smile and he laughs.

"It's one of the things I love most about you. You take no bullshit, and you know what you want," he tells me.

"Most men would be scared off by that," I say.

"Good job I'm not most men then."

"I love you, Jesse."

"And I will always remember how lucky I am to have you say those words to me. I love you too, Natalie, always."

CHAPTER TWENTY-THREE

Jesse

Monday morning, and I stand at the front of the class, looking at my students, trying not to stare daggers at Drake McCoy. He's been sitting there smirking since he walked into my class and sat his ass down. What I wouldn't give to wipe that smug-ass grin from his face.

I haven't had a chance to catch up with Natalie yet. Yesterday was a shitty day where I didn't hear a thing from her and where I was left wondering what the hell was going on. I can only assume that she had to deal with her parents, but it doesn't ease my racing thoughts that she hasn't shown up for class today.

I racked my brain for a way to make this all better, but I came up with absolutely fucking nothing, and I feel like a goddamn failure. I'm a man who doesn't shy away from shit that needs to be sorted, but how in the hell am I going to get near Joey Valentine to speak to him? Brody was my only option, and that blew up in my face.

As if the heavens heard my call, the door to my class opens, and there stands Joey Valentine. Fuck. Maybe it wasn't the heavens that heard my call, but the devil himself.

"Professor Marks, a word," Joey says, his voice seeming to boom around the room, silencing the few students that were talking amongst themselves.

Out of the corner of my eye, I see Drake's smirk turn into a smile. Wanker.

"Class, if you'll excuse me for a few moments, turn to the Carlton case on page fifty-three and start reading. I won't be long," I announce before turning and making my way over to the door.

Joey has already disappeared from sight, and as I exit the lecture room and shut the door behind me, I turn to see that Natalie is stood at the end of the corridor, with her mother, both of them watching me.

I suddenly feel very out of my depth, but my love for Natalie outweighs the nerves I feel right now, and I dare anyone to try call me a pussy at this moment in time because even the baddest of men would feel some unease being around two legends from the underworld. And a weaker man would run, but I am not weak. If this is what I think it is, then I am ready to take my punishment, and I would take it over and over again. Every second of being with Natalie has been worth whatever shitstorm is about to be thrown my way.

I follow Joey until we come to a stop in front of Natalie and her mother.

"Professor Marks," Paige says, holding out her perfectly manicured hand for me to shake.

"Mrs Valentine," I say with a nod of my head as I shake her hand. "Natalie," I greet as I turn my attention to her. "Is everything okay?"

"No, everything is not okay," Joey says from beside me. "But I think talking in private would be best."

"My office is just down the corridor, please, follow me," I say as I move past them and walk as casually as I can to my office.

With every footstep, I feel like I am about to meet my goddamn maker. Maybe I deserve whatever they are about to do? I mean, I fell in love with a student, a fucking student, and I let my overwhelming love for a woman eradicate any rational thought.

I reach my office and open the door, standing back and gesturing for the three of them to enter first. Joey takes the lead, Paige behind him, and Natalie last. As she passes me, she gives me small smile and quickly follows her parents.

I say one last silent prayer as I enter my office and close the door.

Doomsday has arrived.

CHAPTER TWENTY-FOUR

Natalie

I FIGHT the urge to smirk at the fact that Jesse is trying to hide that he looks like he is shitting broken glass. I mean, I know that he is a guy who can take care of himself, but my parents are the fucking masters at intimidation, and even though Jesse would never be able to guess what is about to happen, the intimidation tactic seems to be having an effect on my guy.

I'm going to give him shit about this moment for many years.

"Please, take a seat," Jesse says as he gestures to the chairs in front of his desk. There are only two, but before I can grab myself another chair from the corner of the room, Jesse has already done it, placing it beside the chair my mum has sat in.

"Thank you," I say as I sit down and try to act casual as fuck. I mean, Jesse makes my skin tingle for fuck's sake, so keeping the way he makes me feel under wraps from my parents isn't easy.

Jesse takes his seat on the other side of his desk, and damn if his arms straining inside of his shirt don't make me want to rip the damn fabric off of him.

"So, Mr and Mrs Valentine, what can I do for you?" Jesse says as he sits forwards in his chair, his elbows resting on his desk, and his fingers linked together in front of him.

"I won't beat around the bush here, so I'll get straight to the point," my dad says, all business-like. "Over the weekend, my daughter was attacked as you can see from the bruise and cut on her lip. We currently don't know who did it, and this is the only place that I am unable to protect her, so that is why we are coming to you." I know that coming here is killing my dad on the inside, my mum too. They don't ask for help, but Uni is the one place that they can't look after me. Not that I need looking after, but still, I know how they work, and I know they only care about my safety.

"Go on," Jesse says, sitting forward in his seat more, his eagerness for more information evident and I hope my parents don't read too much into it. My dad may be doing the talking, but my mum is watching Jesse like a hawk. She's good at getting a read on people, and I start to feel slightly panicky.

"We want you to look out for anyone that may be acting suspicious around Natalie in your lectures," my dad continues. "We will find out who did this, and with your help here, we may be able to find out a little bit quicker."

Jesse looks from my dad to my mum, and then to me. I can already see the fierce determination in his eyes, and I know that he wants to tell my parents that he knows who did it, but I try to give him a warning look without moving my face too much. Christ, what a test of our communication this will be. I plead with my eyes for him to stay quiet. I need my plan to be in place, I want to be the one to bring Drake down and send a message to others that my parents aren't the only Valentine's to be wary of.

Time seems to slow as I grow more tense. Fuck, what a way to start Monday.

"I will do all that I can to make sure that Natalie is safe," Jesse says, returning his gaze back to my dad.

"Good," my dad responds before reaching into the inside pocket of his suit jacket to pull out his business card, which he places on Jesse's desk. Jesse looks to the card and then nods his head. "I think we're done here," my dad announces before standing up and looking to my mum as he buttons up his suit jacket.

My mum stands, her eyes still fixed on Jesse. "Well, it was a pleasure meeting you, Professor Marks," she says as she holds her hand out for him to shake. Jesse stands and reaches across the desk, shakes her hand and then my dad's.

"Anytime, Jesse," my dad says, using Jesse's first name rather than his professional name, reiterating the fact that Jesse is to call him at any time of the day or night. It's another intimidation tactic, the way my dad leans in, the way he shakes his hand with controlled force, the way in which he speaks, the danger lurking in just those two words alone. He's trusting him with my safety because I flat-out refused to stop coming to Uni.

Jesse nods and then my parents turn to me, both of them leaning down in turn to place a kiss on the top of my head.

"We'll see you later," my mum says as she gives me a smile.

"We assume you will escort Natalie to class?" I hear my dad say from behind my mum.

"Of course," Jesse replies, and I feel a flutter of excitement inside of me that we are going to have a few minutes alone together once my parents leave.

My mum moves and my dad leans down, placing a kiss on my cheek. "Stay safe, baby girl."

"Stop worrying, I'm fine," I reply, wanting to ease his worry, which I know is absolutely pointless, but still. "See you at home."

Dad smiles at me and then he's following my mum out of here, closing the door behind them.

Jesse sits back down in his chair, watching me, his eyes holding mine.

"You okay over there?" I say with a side-smile.

"At the risk of looking like a pussy, I thought I was about to have my ass handed to me, if I'm being honest," he replies, leaning back in his chair and letting out a sigh of relief.

"I know, I could tell," I say as I stand up and walk to his side of the desk. He moves back, allowing me to slide in front of him, my legs going either side of his, my hands supporting me as I perch on the edge of his desk and lean back slightly.

Jesse's eyes turn dark as he moves forward, his legs moving between mine. He's still sat down, but he reaches up with his hand and cups the side of my face.

"I thought I was about to lose you, Natalie," he says, and fuck if the emotion in his voice doesn't make a lump form in my throat.

I lean down, resting my forehead against his. "Jesse," I whisper before his lips lock with mine, softly, slowly, lovingly. I can feel everything as his tongue caresses mine. The love, the need, the fucking urgency for us to remain as one. "I love you," I say against his lips.

"God, every time I hear you say that it makes me feel like a fucking teenager," Jesse says, and I chuckle. He pulls his head back, his gorgeous eyes shining with love for me.

"How so?" I ask, because I genuinely enjoy fucking with him every now and then, keeps things fresh.

He sighs and shakes his head. "Never had so much excitement in my dick, Natalie."

I laugh. "Is that how teenage boys think?"

"With their dick? Of course. But there is a clear difference here," he says and then he's standing, caging me against the desk with his arms going either side of me, and it sends a delicious shiver racing through me.

"And what's that?" I say, my voice quiet.

"I am not a boy, and I have no problem admitting how much I fucking love you. Because I do. I love you, Natalie, more than you could ever imagine... but at the same time, the love I feel for you is dangerous. I have never experienced this before, it's changed me, and I wouldn't even question killing for you or dying for you. I would do it every time, because you're mine and you've woken something inside of me that I can't shut off."

I grab his face with both of my hands, cupping his cheeks as I look him square in the eyes.

"I like danger, and there is no question that we belong together, Jesse. We're starting a new chapter in our lives that neither of us expected, and I love the unexpected," I tell him. "And if you ever did have to kill for me, you know I have access to the best clean-up crew around," I finish, injecting a little humour and Jesse barks out a laugh as he throws his head back.

"Forever," I say, once his eyes are back on mine.

"Forever," he confirms with a nod of his head, and damn if it doesn't make me love him more.

CHAPTER TWENTY-FIVE

Natalie

"Baby girl," Drake sneers as I feel him skulking behind me as I head for lunch. My skin crawls having him so close, but I know that it is only a matter of time before I take this asshole down, so I keep my cool and carry on walking.

He falls into step beside me. "That's quite an impressive cut on your lip," he says, and I can hear the smugness in his voice.

I hold my head high, not even turning to look at him.

"Ah, what's the matter? Don't you wanna talk to me, Natalie?" he says, goading me, trying to push my buttons. I fucking hate him with a passion.

"Come on, you can't still be mad at me?" he continues. "I thought you would have gotten over it by now, but I guess when something happens it makes you realise what you truly want, huh?" he says, and out of the corner of my eye, I see him move his hand to his crotch, grabbing it, a smirk on his face. Ugh. Does this kind of shit ever really work on a female?

I mean, I get that exuding male dominance can be a turn on, but fuck, this is just plain embarrassing for him. I guess that's why he has made sure to get me on my own, so he doesn't look like a complete twat in front of his groupies when I call him out on his bullshit in exactly three... two... one...

"Why don't you go spout your bullshit to someone who gives a damn, Drake?" I say, trying to keep my voice as calm as possible.

"And she speaks. I'm honoured," he says sarcastically.

"You fucking should be," I mutter quietly.

"Don't be like that, Nat," he says as he slings his arm around my shoulders. I shrug him off and finally stop walking and turn to look at him, my disgust for him clear on my face.

"Don't touch me," I say, my teeth gritted together.

"Or what?" he says as he steps towards me, backing me against a wall. Fuck. Last time I was against a wall with this fucker, it didn't end so well for me.

I narrow my eyes, not backing down.

"Or I'm going make you wish that you had never been born," I threaten. But it's not a threat. I'm going to make him pay for what he's done.

He laughs in my face. "You haven't got the minerals, baby girl." Ugh.

"Don't test me, asshole."

"Ooo, and what are you gonna do, huh? Set your big, bad daddy on me?"

Now it's my turn to laugh at him. "I don't need my dad to fight my battles, Drake."

"You know, when you speak to me like that, it gets me all hot," he says as he licks his lips. What I wouldn't give to cut the fucker's tongue off right now. I'd frame it and hang it on the goddamn wall.

He moves his arms, so his hands are pressed against the wall and he's caging me in. But I'm prepared this time, with a pocket-knife tucked into the back of my jeans. I move my hand behind me whilst Drake places his lips by my ear.

"You know, Natalie, you really should give up the old man dick and take a ride on mine. It would do wonders for all of that stress that seems to plague you—" His words die on his lips when he feels the cool blade of my knife pressing against his Adam's apple.

"The only reason you were able to do anything the last time, Drake, is because I was drunk and unprepared, but make no mistake, I will never be unprepared again." I see him gulp and I smile. Good. The fucker deserves to sweat a little bit. "Now, let me make this very clear so that even you will understand," I start as I push the blade against his skin a little bit more.

"I am going to forget about this little chat because, honestly, you bore the fucking ass off of me. Your threats mean shit, your advances don't scare me, and I am more than ready to go to fucking war with you, McCoy."

"You haven't got the balls," he whispers, but his words hold no grounds, and the sweat starts to trickle down his forehead.

"I may not have actual balls, but don't think for one minute that I won't gut you like a fucking fish. I have the best access to hiding your body, making sure you are never to be found again, and don't you ever forget it," I sneer.

"And what about your dirty little secret?" he says, betting on his bargaining chip.

"Ha. I have no dirty secret, but you have plenty," I retort.

"You mean to tell me that everyone knows about you and the Professor?" he says, and I see the glint in his eye when he thinks that he has got me. Wrong.

"I do not answer to you, Drake, and the sooner you remember that the better it will be."

"Funny, because I could have sworn that you would want

to keep that secret under wraps," he says, but he doesn't look so sure of himself anymore. I nick his skin with the knife and he hisses, a tiny drop of blood falling down his neck.

"I told you not to push me," I tell him, my eyes boring into his.

"You're gonna regret that," he says.

"Not as much as you will."

I hold his stare until he backs away, putting his fingers to his neck and pulling them away with a tiny drop of blood on them.

"This is going to be fun," he says with a smirk before he turns and walks off, disappearing through the door that leads to the canteen.

I put my knife away as if nothing has happened and I calmly follow the path that Drake has just taken.

Pulling my phone out of my pocket, I text Marshall, telling him that we need a new plan. There is no way that I can offer myself up as the bait, Drake would never believe that I was giving into him in a million years, and I can't bring myself to try and act like I want to seduce his disgusting ass.

Marshall texts back straight away, telling me to meet him at Tulip when Uni is finished for the day.

I need to get my thinking cap on, and I need to do it quick.

CHAPTER TWENTY-SIX

Jesse

I'VE BEEN TRYING to phone Natalie since Uni ended, but her phone keeps going to voicemail.

Fuck.

I saw Drake speaking to her earlier from the window in the staff room, but I couldn't go out there and do anything about it without drawing attention to myself as Mrs Dudley was chuntering away in my ear, and she is the biggest gossip of the fucking school. She's also been trying to get into my pants since she started working here six months ago. No fucking thank you.

So as she waffled on about God knows what—because I wasn't listening—Natalie was dealing with that asshole yet again. I tried to find her after lunch, but with lectures this afternoon, I was unable to catch up with her. And now, here I am, sat in my car, trying to get in touch with her.

I feel restless.

I know something isn't right.

I just don't know what I can do because I have no idea what Natalie's plan is or what Drake is trying to achieve by being a massive pain in the ass.

I take a deep breath and lean my head back against the seat.

Think, Jesse, think. Where could Natalie be?

I could try her house, but if she were there, I'm pretty sure she would be picking up the phone to me.

I could try to get hold of Sophia, but that just doesn't feel right and I'm not comfortable with contacting her, never mind the fucking ethics involved in that. I mean, I've crossed the line irreparably with Natalie, but I don't need to bring anymore shit to my door by contacting another student.

I watch as students filter out of the car park after having a chat before making their way home, and then it hits me out of nowhere.

Tulip.

That's where she'll be.

Her run-in with Drake will have sent her to speak to Marshall.

I start the car, the engine roaring as I screech out of the car park, not giving one single fuck about the shocked looks I'm getting from the students that are leaving the grounds.

I PULL up outside Tulip and turn the engine off. I know that I could be walking into a situation where I put the kiss of death on my life, but I don't care. All I want to do is make sure Natalie is okay.

I slam the car door shut after getting out and march to the entrance of Tulip.

I am about to bang on the door when it opens, but there doesn't appear to be anyone stood behind it.

I cautiously take a step inside, and then another until I am in a corridor, the door closing behind me.

What the fuck?

There's no one around and I strain my ears, but it's quiet. An eerie feeling creeps over me, but I push it away. I need to find Natalie.

I turn left down the corridor and keep my ears pricked, but let's face it, the people inside of here are the fucking masters at sneaking up on people, so if they wanted to come at me, I'd probably be on my fucking ass and have a gun held to my head before I could actually do anything. I am not a man to go down without a fight, but when it comes to dealing with members of the underworld, I am at a severe disadvantage.

I turn left and make my way up some steps, which lead to the next level and is just as plush as the ground floor. I mean, the colours are rich, the floors are gleaming, and the lighting isn't too harsh but it's also not too dim. I see a door to the left, in the middle of the corridor, so I make my way there and try to listen for voices, but again, there is nothing. Figuring that I may possibly die here today anyway, I take my chances and open the door slowly.

And what I see on the other side is Natalie, sat in a chair to the side of a large desk, one leg crossed over the other and a beaming smile on her face. Opening the door further, I see a guy sat behind the desk, his eyes fixed on me, his face deadpan.

I have no idea what to fucking do here, but I don't have to try and figure it out because the guy behind the desk speaks.

"Well, you made it this far, Professor, so you do have some balls. You may as well shut the damn door and take a seat," he says. I want to say something back to him, but I don't. This is Natalie's world, and right now, I'm a trespasser. I haven't earnt my right to be here… yet.

"Take a seat," Natalie says as she points to the chair in front of the desk, giving me her come-fuck-me eyes. *Later, baby.*

I give her a side-smile and take a seat, leaning back, trying to act casual as fuck whereas, really, I'm a little goddamn nervous.

"Jesse, this is Marshall. Marshall, this is Jesse," Natalie says, and I nod at Marshall as he continues to stare at me. He's so young. I expected him to be older for some reason, I don't know why. I mean, Natalie hasn't really told me that much about him, so I really have nothing to go on about how this is going to go down.

"Pleasure to meet you, Marshall," I say, attempting to get some sort of ice broken and some kind of conversation started here. I don't like how tense it all feels.

"Jesus, Natty, he's old as fuck," Marshall says as he leans back in his chair and looks away from me.

I sit there, shocked to hell about what he just said whilst Natalie chuckles.

"Play nice, Marshall," Natalie says when she has finished laughing at my expense. I don't give a fuck that she's laughing, I'm just glad to see that she is okay.

"Pleasure to meet you?" Marshall questions, repeating my words from a few moments ago. "I mean, come on, Natty, what the fuck?" he says before turning his attention back to me. "Seriously, dude, if you're gonna come around here, you don't need to be putting on any airs and graces. Just a simple 'hello' or 'hey' will suffice."

I'm unsure what to say. Is this guy fucking with me?

"Ignore him," Natalie says with a roll of her eyes as she gets up and comes over to me, leaning down and giving me a light kiss on the lips. *What the fuck?*

"Oh, Natty, seriously? Do you have to do that?" Marshall

says and Natalie moves back from me and winks before taking her seat again.

"Oh please, you're going to cringe out over me kissing my boyfriend when you have a different girl sucking your dick in here every night?" Natalie says, and damn if I don't feel a little awkward right now.

"I don't do it in front of you," Marshall argues.

"No, but you always forget to lock the fucking door," Natalie retorts.

What the fuck have I walked in on?

They both pause for a second and turn to look at me, and then Marshall starts to laugh.

I look at him, feeling so out of my depth it is ridiculous. I almost wish some fucker had jumped me so I would have known how to react.

"Jesus, Nat, he scares easy, huh?" Marshall says and then he starts to smirk. "Fucking perfect, this is going to be fun."

"Cut it out, Marshall," Natalie scolds him before turning back to me. "Jesse, take no notice of him, he's a fucking joker and then some."

"Hey," Marshall says loudly, sitting forwards in his seat. "I may be the joker, but who do you come to when you need shit fucked up?"

Natalie sighs and takes a deep breath, ignoring him and keeping her attention on me. "You okay over there?" she asks me.

Am I okay?

Is she for real?

No, I'm not okay. I have no clue what the fuck is going on.

I just nod at her, unable to actually form any words for the moment.

"How did you know to find me here?" she asks.

I clear my throat to speak. "I tried to call you, but when it kept going to voicemail, I ran through the options of where you might be, and this is the conclusion I came to seeing as I saw your run in with McCoy today," I tell her.

"You saw?" she says with one eyebrow raised and a side-smile on her face. She doesn't look shocked, she looks impressed.

"I did. What the hell did he want?" I ask her, completely ignoring Marshall because he doesn't fucking matter right now.

"He was just being his usual charming self," she says sarcastically.

"I need more than that, Natalie," I tell her, my eyes boring into hers. I will not back down here, I've been kept in the dark for too long already, and I need more from her.

"He was goading me, I pulled my pocketknife out, held it against his throat, drew a little blood and then told him that he would live to regret what he had done," she says with a shrug of her shoulders.

"Oh, so nothing major then?" I say sarcastically. "For fuck's sake, Natalie, you need to keep me in the goddamn loop."

"There isn't anything you can do, Jesse," she says softly, and I can see that she knows how frustrating this is for me.

"That's because you don't let me," I say, not backing down.

"If you were to get involved, you know what would happen."

"And I have already told you, I don't care."

"And I do," she argues back, her eyes blazing as are mine.

We hold each other's stare for a beat before I hear Marshall speak.

"Hmm, interesting," he ponders as he sits there, looking between the two of us.

"What is?" Natalie snaps.

"Well, my dear Natty, it seems you have underestimated Professor Marks." He exaggerates the Professor part slightly as if to nail home the fact that I have totally crossed the line.

"What?" she says, frowning.

"You're not a stupid woman, Natalie, so don't sit there and act all bloody ignorant," Marshall replies. "Even I can see that he wants to help you, and for that alone, I won't chop his dick up and serve it up to your dad."

Chop my dick off? Jesus Christ.

"He can't be involved, Marshall," Natalie says.

"Like fuck I can't," I chime in. "I want to help, I need to help, stop pushing me away," I insist.

"See?" Marshall says with a casual wave of his hand. He sits forward and braces his elbows on the desk. "The way I see it, he already is involved whether he likes it or not, but the fact that he wants to come on board just proves that he's not a goddamn wimp."

"He can't, Marshall," Natalie says, her voice a little bit quieter than before.

"Don't speak about me like I'm not even here," I say, my irritation growing the longer she keeps trying to protect me, because that is what she thinks she is doing, protecting me, and I don't bloody want it or need it.

"Sorry, Jesse, but you're not thinking clearly," she says.

"I am. I've never been as clear in thought as I am at this moment in time," I reply. "I already told you, I don't give a shit about my teaching career, all I give a shit about is you." My passion for her shows in my words. "I fucking love you, Natalie, and I'm ready to do whatever it takes to be with you properly, without all the cloak and dagger stuff, and if that means coming on board with whatever plan you have to take down Drake, then count me the fuck in." My chest heaves as I finish my rant.

Natalie's eyes glisten, a small smile on her face.

A few moments of silence pass, and then I am asked a question that is going to absolutely change my life.

"You all in?" Marshall asks and I turn to him, ignoring the silent plea in Natalie's eyes to stay away from whatever danger may await us all.

I clench my jaw and lean forwards, my eyes not leaving Marshall's, and I utter the words that I can never take back.

"I'm all in."

CHAPTER TWENTY-SEVEN

Natalie

What the hell?

I know that Jesse loves me, and I know that he said before that he wanted to be there for me, to help me, to always be my ride or die, but making a deal with Marshall has just sealed his fate.

The only way he will leave this world now is dead.

And I am fucking panicking.

"Jesse, stop it," I say as the panic runs through me. I don't want to ever lose him, and he knows nothing of what my family are capable of. Sure, he's heard the stories, but fuck, I don't want him to disappear because he doesn't play ball.

"Stop what?" he replies, his face stoic.

"Forgive me for what I am about to say, but you are a goddamn teacher. You don't have the first idea about what you are getting yourself into—"

"Don't underestimate me, Natalie," he interrupts.

"I don't underestimate you, but Jesus Christ, Jesse, you've

just agreed to basically sign your life away by saying you're all in!" I exclaim as I stand up and start pacing the floor. "You don't have the first clue how this world works."

"Enlighten me then," he replies.

"Calm down, Natty," Marshall chimes in.

"Calm down? Fucking calm down?" I seethe. "How can I be calm when he wants to try and learn what we've been learning our whole lives?"

"I am not fucking stupid, Natalie, and I am not totally in the dark about how things work around here," Jesse says, his jaw clenched, his eyes narrowing. "I have a friend that runs drugs for Meghan and Miles."

At this piece of information, I stop pacing and Marshall scoots forwards even more in his seat, his eyes lighting up.

"Who?" Marshall asks Jesse.

Jesse smirks. "Now that would be telling, and I'm not about to betray him by giving you a name."

If this were a test, then he would absolutely fucking pass.

Marshall contemplates his words before he breaks into a grin. "I like you, despite the fact that you've been fucking Natalie in unethical circumstances."

I roll my eyes at the crudeness of his words. Subtlety has never been Marshall's strong point.

"Now, are you going to tell me what the plan is? Or am I going to have to keep on convincing you that I am all fucking in," Jesse says, directing his words to me, his eyes blazing with the love that he holds for me.

I walk over to him, slowly, until I am leaning down, my face level with his. I hold his stare for a beat before I lightly brush my lips over his, moving them to his ear and whispering, "I love you."

When I pull back, he moves his hand and grabs me by the nape of my neck, tilting me so my forehead rests against his.

"Never forget that you're my always, Natalie. I would die

for you, and if that is what I have to do, then so fucking be it," he says in the sexiest voice I have ever heard him use. Dear God, my pussy is tingling with desire for this man. "I don't give a shit about how we started out; all I care about is that we are a team."

"But I don't want to lose you," I whisper, the emotion of the moment getting to me.

"You won't."

"You can't be sure of that," I tell him. "This world is cruel and heartless, Jesse."

"Then I guess I'll just have to become as cruel and heartless as some of the assholes that try to come between us," he tells me. "But I can promise you that I will never be ruthless with you. You are my everything, and I don't give a shit if that sounds corny, it's the absolute truth. I fucking love you, and that will never change."

And there we have it.

Jesse declaring his undying love for me, regardless of the fact that Marshall is in the room with us. I wish he wasn't here so I could ride Jesse's cock right now, but that will have to wait until later.

I push my lips against his as his grip on my nape tightens. So fucking hot.

We break apart a few moments later and I smile. "You're going to get so lucky later."

"I was counting on it," he says and gives me his gorgeous smile that makes me feel weak at the knees.

I hear Marshall clear his throat and I move away, Jesse's hand falling from my nape.

"If you two have quite finished," Marshall starts, shifting in his seat. "Even though that is one of the most passionate displays I've seen in quite some time, we have business to discuss, so shall we get on with it?" he says as he gestures for me to return to my seat. I move away from Jesse and sit down, crossing one leg over the other and leaning back in my chair.

"So, as it stands, the plan is a bit..."

"Fucked," Marshall says, finishing my sentence.

"How so?" Jesse asks.

Marshall scoffs and Jesse looks at both of us in question.

"You wanna tell him?" Marshall says to me, and I inwardly cringe because he is not going to like hearing this one little bit.

"Well, the original plan was to use myself as the bait, lure him in, make him think I was seducing him and get him confessing to some of the shit he's done whilst recording it so we had proof to bargain with," I start, and I can see that he is flabbergasted that I would even suggest something like this in the first place. "But I can't do it, nor do I want to," I continue.

"I should think not," Jesse says, unable to keep quiet any longer. "Even I can see the flaws in that plan, but the biggest one is that you are in no way using yourself as fucking bait, Natalie, no matter who you are going up against."

"Yes, I get that, hence why we need a new plan," I respond, and Jesse seems to simmer down ever so slightly.

"You don't have another idea of how to nail this bastard?" Jesse asks, and I feel like a fucking failure. I should have a plan, but I don't because my mind is consumed with all things Jesse when I should be concentrating on how to get rid of Drake fucking McCoy.

"Shocking, isn't it?" Marshall says as he looks at Jesse. "I mean, she's always got a plan, no matter what, but I guess her head is a little clouded at the moment..." Marshall's voice fades off and he smiles because he loves giving me shit at times.

Jesse moves his arms out either side of him, holding them open as he says, "Use me."

Marshall and I stare at him, waiting for him to expand. He's made it clear that he wants to be here and there's no turning back, so I need to make peace with it and accept that he is one of us now.

"He won't suspect me because of my job," Jesse clarifies. "I'll stay as a Professor until Drake is dealt with, and then I'll leave."

My eyes widen in shock. "You can't leave."

"Why not?"

"It's your career, Jesse."

"Not anymore."

"Oh for—"

"Wait, wait, wait," Marshall says, holding his hand up to silence us. "He's got a point."

I roll my eyes and flop back in my chair, knowing that I will have already lost this argument.

"He may suspect something to start with, but it wouldn't hold as much grounds as it would if Natalie or I went to face-off with him..." I can see Marshall working something out in his mind. "And I don't think we need some drastic plan, I just think we need to scare him, fuck him up a little bit."

"Fuck him up a little bit?" Jesse asks.

I sigh. "I may have forgotten to mention that Marshall is the fucking psycho of the group. He likes to play with knives and screwdrivers, and anything that can cause maximum pain."

"Just some good old-fashioned slicing and dicing to get the point across," Marshall confirms but we both know he takes it to the next level, always has done, and it ensures that people don't piss him off a second time.

I can see Jesse's eyes widen slightly.

I smirk. "Aren't you glad you decided to be all in?"

CHAPTER TWENTY-EIGHT

Jesse

AFTER LEAVING TULIP, I drove back to my place, and now, here I stand, watching the kettle boil as if a fucking cup of tea is going to fix everything. How very British of me. Natalie stands next to me, her silence making me feel anxious.

She decided to follow me back to my place, and I had plans to fuck the life out of her, but my mind has been working overtime and I can't seem to stop it from thinking of everything that was discussed.

Revenge.
Plan.
Pain.
Drake.
Cut.
Slice.
Pay.
Fuck.
It's all there, whirring around on a loop.

"Jesse," Natalie says as I feel her hand rest on my shoulder, her fingers digging in slightly as they move in slow circles. I bet she can feel the fucking knot beneath my skin. As if she clarifies that she can, she moves to stand behind me, putting her free hand on my other shoulder and massaging both of them in sync. I close my eyes and let my head fall back slightly. It feels good as she digs her fingers into my skin.

"You know that we will always have your back, don't you?" she says as if needing to make me believe that I am not about to get fed to the wolves.

"And if you want to back out—" I don't even let her finish that sentence. I turn around, cutting her off and then I'm pinning her against the wall, her arms above her head, her back connecting with a low thud.

"I am not backing out of anything," I assure her, her head tilted slightly so she is looking in my eyes.

"Then why are you so tense?" she asks me, her eyes blazing as I move my body closer to hers, making sure our chests are rubbing together, not a slither of space between us.

"You really want to know?" I say as I move my head down and lightly trace my nose over her skin before stopping by her ear.

"Yes."

"I'm tense because I didn't realise how much I'm going to enjoy ripping Drake apart. I didn't expect to feel this adrenaline pulsing through me at the mere thought. And knowing that you will have my back to help clean up and cover up"—I move from her ear, back across her cheek and stop just in front of her lips—"turns me the fuck on," I growl before my lips crash down on hers. It's true, I do feel turned on because it's so incredibly sexy that she is going to be a part of this with me, and I am now a part of her world. That's why I feel anxious, because I'm not used to feeling this way about inflicting violence. Maybe I am more like them than I ever thought?

From what I know though, they've only ever gone after people when there has been a genuine reason. The Valentine's don't hurt people just for fun, they do it to prove a point and to make clear that they will not have anyone fuck up their shit in any way whatsoever.

I bite Natalie's bottom lip, becoming fucking feral as I lift her up, my fingers sinking into the softness of her ass cheeks, her legs linking around me. Her hands are resting on my shoulders, and then they are at the back of my neck, in my hair, pulling, tugging, and it feels so damn good.

I growl and push against her, holding her in place against the wall as I move my hands down her arms, down her sides, and then let my fingers grip the front of her shirt before I tear it open, the buttons flying in different directions as I feast my eyes upon her black lace bra, which barely covers her nipples. Fucking beautiful.

I lower my lips to her skin, grazing my teeth along her bra line, letting my tongue dart out to lick her nipples through the fabric. She gasps and I can no longer control the animal inside of me that wants to fuck her senseless.

I pull her bra down with my teeth, and then my lips cover her nipple as I tease her with my tongue, swirling it around. The mid-length skirt she is wearing allows me to move my fingers to her knickers which are already wet. I do that to her. Me. All fucking me, and it is the best feeling in the world.

I run my fingers up and down, hearing her gasp again. Her legs are still locked around me, giving me the perfect angle to pull her knickers to the side as I push two fingers inside of her. She moans, her fingers digging into my shoulders and I move mine in and out of her, quick and hard. Her wetness coats me as I drive my fingers inside of her, and I don't stop as I move us from the wall and carry her up the stairs. She clings onto me, her head falling to my shoulder as I let my other hand cup her ass, my forefinger nudging between her cheeks, teasing her.

I reach my bedroom and kick the door open before I throw her on the bed, her gorgeous tits bouncing as she hits the mattress. Her hair is a little messy and her eyes have a look that says she can't live without my touch. Perfect.

I quickly rid myself of my clothes, leaving them in a heap on the floor before I climb over her, pushing her skirt up and ripping her knickers off, throwing them fuck knows where. Where her knickers land is the last thing on my mind right now.

"Jesse," she pants, but I'm not in the mood to talk. I'm in the mood to taste her, so I lean down and bury my tongue in her pussy as she screams out in pleasure. I fuck her with my tongue whilst my thumb rubs circles on her clit. I return my other hand to her ass and press gently against her opening as her legs start to tremble.

"Oh my fu—" Her words are cut off as I insert my finger and suck her clit. Her back arches and damn if she doesn't look like the hottest fucking woman to have ever walked the earth. And when I use my free hand to slide two fingers inside of her, it's like I press the fucking detonator as she screams out, her hands moving to grip my hair as she rides her release. And I do not let up one little bit. I suck harder, move my fingers in and out quicker and take every-fucking-thing she has to give.

I am a greedy bastard, and I need it all.

Her whole body trembles but I am nowhere near done with her yet. I quickly rip my fingers and my mouth from her before I flip her over, lifting her ass in the air and bury my dick deep inside of her.

The feeling of her wrapped around me is pure heaven, and I pound into her, deep and fast. Her body doesn't have time to recover from her first orgasm as I feel her walls tighten around me already. It spurs me on, and I plunge into her over and over again whilst reaching for her breasts, letting my fingers play with her nipples, my lips trailing kisses over her back.

As she moans loudly and I feel her walls tighten more, I move one of my hands and wrap her hair around it, allowing me to pull her head back and place my lips by her ear as I grunt out the words, "I. Fucking. Love. You." And that does it. As I spear into her, she lets go and screams out my name, over and over again. Wish I'd recorded that shit because fuck if her voice doesn't do things to me. I hold her in place as I race to my release, the world shifting as I explode inside of her, the roar that leaves me louder than her screams.

And when I know that we are both spent from a fucking of a lifetime, we collapse on the bed, me on top of her, my chest to her back. I don't put all of my weight on her, but I cage her in because she is mine. Mine to protect, mine to love, mine to worship every damn day.

I move her hair to the side and place light kisses on the back of her neck as she tries to catch her breath.

"Jesse," she whispers a few moments later.

"Hmm?" I mumble, still mesmerised by the fact that I get to touch her at all.

I feel her body move beneath me as she tries to turn around. I lift my body up, allowing her to do so, and then she is facing me, her beautiful silver eyes holding mine.

Her hand comes up to my cheek and her fingers brush against my stubble before she lifts her head up and pushes her lips to mine, capturing my tongue with hers, softly, gently and nothing like the pace we were going at only minutes ago. It's a complete contrast and I am here for it.

When she pulls back, resting her head back on the pillow, she looks at me with a sparkle in her eyes.

"Always," she says, and it's like we both know what that means.

Always us.

Always together.

Always a team.

I smile as I say the words back to her, knowing that this means something to us and only us. "Always."

CHAPTER TWENTY-NINE

Natalie

I WALK through the front door of my house feeling a little miserable to be honest. I mean, I've just had the hottest sex ever with the man I want to spend the rest of my life with, and I can't actually be with him right now. I didn't want to leave his place, and I know that he wanted me to stay, but I can't lie to my parents. I don't want to have to tell them I'm staying at Sophia's to cover up the fact that I am with Jesse.

I'm sick of hiding.

I'm tired of keeping it quiet.

I have had enough of skulking in the shadows.

And I am a motherfucking Valentine, and we own our shit when it needs to be owned.

I need to tell them. I need to make them understand what the two of us have together, and I need them to realise that we have a strong bond and the same level of commitment to each other as they do.

Yes, they will be mad.

Yes, they will need time to process it.

But it's time to be truthful with them because my feelings for Jesse are growing stronger with every day that passes.

I also need to tell them about Drake. Jesse and Marshall don't know that I want to tell them about Drake, and Jesse doesn't know I want to tell them about us, because I only made all of these decisions when I was driving home from Jesse's. They are my parents, and I know that even if they are angry with me, they will always have my back... I hope.

I walk to the kitchen, but there is no sign of anyone. I check the lounge, but that's empty too, so I scale the house looking for them.

When there are no signs of life, I head down to the basement where there is a game room and a cinema-type area, and there they are, huddled together underneath a blanket, watching some action film on the big screen.

"Oh, come on, that is so fucking exaggerated," my mum says as she puts a piece of popcorn in her mouth and throws her hands in the air.

"Paige, baby, it's just a film," my dad says whilst chuckling.

"Yes, Joey, I am fully aware, but for fuck's sake, they should really keep to some kind of reality."

"But then it wouldn't be as exciting."

"It can be exciting without all of this ridiculous nonsense," my mum continues, clearly unimpressed with whatever this film is.

"Adrenaline junkies probably live for these kinds of films," my dad says, and I can hear the amusement in his tone.

"Yeah? And sex addicts probably live for the porn, but at least they make it look somewhat realistic."

My dad roars with laughter and my mum chucks a piece of popcorn at him. He takes her hand in his and moves his other hand to her face, brushing her hair behind her shoulder.

"You know I love you," he says to her.

"I know. Ride or die, big guy," she says back with a smile.

"Ride or die," my dad says before he places a kiss on her lips, and that is when I turn around and leave, deciding that this is not the moment to tell them about Jesse or Drake.

Instead, I scribble a note and leave it on the kitchen island telling them that I've gone to Sophia's for the night, and that is actually where I intend on going because I need her to help me, and I'm hoping she's up for the challenge.

"Hey, girl," Sophia says as she answers the door. "Come in." She steps back and I enter her hallway which is cream and grey coloured throughout.

"Are your parent's home?" I ask her and she shakes her head.

"No, they left for Dubai this morning," she says, reminding me that she mentioned that her parents were going away again, because that is all they do. They leave her on her own all the time and act like they can throw money at her to buy her love rather than actually spend time with her.

"Okay, good, because I wanted to make sure no one was around when I spoke to you," I tell her and then I grab her arm, pulling her behind me and slamming the front door shut as I go past.

I walk us into the lounge and over to the sofa.

"Jesus, Natalie, what is going on?" Sophia says as she flops down on the sofa and I let go of her arm.

"Please listen to everything I have to say before you jump in," I tell her because I need to get it all out before she can judge me for jumping in with my feet first.

"O-kay," she says slowly as she gives me a weird look like I have lost my damn mind, which I may well have done since I left my house and came over here.

"Right," I say as I get ready to tell her my plan. "Well, I need to deal with Drake, and I want to do it without Jesse, and I was hoping that you would help me. I want to get him on his own, make him confess to some of the shit he's done, get it on tape and use it against him to keep his mouth shut about me and Jesse."

There. I said it, and I have pretty much gone back to my original plan. It's not the best, but it will work. I know it will. It has to.

"Whoa, whoa, whoa," Sophia says as she holds her hand up, palms facing me. "You are going to have to tell me the whole goddamn story before I even contemplate getting involved in this, Nat."

"Yes, of course," I say and then tell her all about how Jesse showed up at Tulip earlier today and shook hands with the devil himself, also known as Marshall.

"But why do you want to keep him out of it?" she asks.

"Because..." I sigh. "I don't want him to lose his job, Sophia, and I don't want him to get in trouble because of me. I just... I don't know what the fuck to do and this was the only thing I could think of... I don't want to get you involved either, not really," I admit, because as much as I am a Valentine, I am grasping at fucking straws here.

"What is it you want me to do?" she asks.

"I was going to see if you could get Drake to a location on his own, and then I would be waiting there with Marshall because I need his crazy ass with me, and I know that Drake will absolutely know that it is a trap if I try and lure him anywhere," I say with another fucking sigh. I've never been this frustrated in my life.

"It's a pretty loose plan, Nat," she tells me, and I nod.

"I know, just forget I said anything, I need to come up with something better," I say, feeling like a failure as I lean back against the sofa, close my eyes and rub my temples as I feel a headache building.

"Or..." Sophia says, and I pop my eyes back open to look at her. "You could stop feeling so sorry for yourself right about now and we could do your plan and put an end to his threats once and for all."

"You mean... You actually want to do this with me?" I ask her, a little shocked that she is so easily seeming to agree.

"Sure," she replies with a shrug of her shoulders. "I got nothing else to do and I wouldn't mind seeing Drake be brought to his fucking knees for being a sleazy bastard."

We both laugh and then my common sense actually decides to kick in.

"No, I can't let you lure him to me, it's not right and it puts you at risk," I say, shaking my head and wishing that I had never mentioned anything in the first place.

I'm so stupid for even saying anything. Damn, being in love really does mess with your head, it makes your mind hazy, and it will ensure that you do anything possible for the other person even if the decisions are questionable.

"Natalie," she starts, putting her hand over mine as it rests on the sofa beside my leg. "You are my best friend, and I want to help you. You would help me if it was the other way around."

"That's different though and you know it," I say, giving her a knowing look.

"I don't care. I want to do this, Nat, and you are not going to sit there and feel guilty about it," she tells me, and I can't help but laugh at her finger pointing at my face. "Now, make the call to Marshall and let's get ourselves ready."

"You want to do it right now?" I ask in shock as she stands up and straightens her shirt.

"Of course. No time like the present," she says as she

shrugs her shoulders and flounces off in the direction of her bedroom.

"Well. Damn," I whisper as I pull my phone out of my pocket and dial Marshall's number. I underestimated Sophia.

"Natty, talk to me," Marshall says as he answers the phone.

"One hour."

"When and where?" he asks me. He doesn't need me to expand. If I give him an amount of time, he knows what that means.

"You at Tulip?" I ask him.

"Yup."

"Then you need to go nowhere because we're coming to you."

"We?" he asks.

"Me, Sophia and Drake," I tell him.

"No Jesse?" he asks.

"No. He doesn't know about any of this."

He chuckles down the phone. "I knew you wouldn't let him get involved."

"What can I say? With a friend who's willing to lure Drake to us and a psycho cousin who will be ready to slice and dice at a moment's notice, there is no need to involve him."

"It's been a long time since I was allowed to play, Natty," he says, and I can already hear the excitement in his voice at finally unleashing his bad side.

"Well, tonight you get to have your fun, but I get to have mine first. I'm gonna make that fucker confess to every little thing he's ever done, and then I'm going to play that shit on a loop if he dares to come for me again." I can feel the anger burning inside of me. Drake fucking McCoy will wish that he had never stepped onto my radar. He may have gotten a few lucky hits in the last time, but this time he'll be lucky to fucking breathe by the time I'm done with him.

CHAPTER THIRTY

Natalie

I'M WATCHING the monitors in Marshall's office, my eyes focussed on the front doors as Sophia walks in with Drake behind her.

I have to admit, I had my doubts about her getting him here, but I shouldn't have because he looks positively mesmerised as he follows her, his eyes on her ass as she sashays her way into the club and walks past the bar, heading for the corridor that leads to this room. Drake doesn't even bat an eyelid as I watch him follow her up the steps. In about five seconds, Sophia will be opening the door to this room. And in about ten seconds, Drake is going to wish that he had never fucked with me.

One...
Two...
Three...
Four...

Five…

The handle turns and the door opens, Drake's back is to me as Sophia has her hand on his chest and makes him back further into the room. It's dark in here and I am sat behind Marshall's desk, the only light flickering from the monitors that I no longer need to watch. I quickly flick the monitors off and sit silently as Sophia acts out the role of a lifetime.

"I must say, Sophia, I never expected to find myself alone in a room with you, and here of all places," Drake says as she manoeuvres him towards the sofa that Marshall regularly gets his dick sucked on.

"What can I say?" she purrs. "I like to live dangerously."

"I can see that."

"What about you, Drake? Do you like a little danger?" she asks as she nudges him, and he falls backwards onto the sofa.

"I love nothing more," he replies in his sleazy voice. "Why else would I come here with you? I mean, I'm not exactly welcome here as you know, but I also know that there is no way I will be kicked out."

"And why is that?" Sophia asks sweetly.

"Because they haven't got the balls and I've got one hell of a secret to unleash if they so much as try," he says. Ugh, asshole thinks he can just rock on in here like he owns us. Big mistake, and that's my cue.

Show time.

With Drake's attention on Sophia, I stand and quietly make my way around the desk. The low thump of the music playing inside the club acts as a mask for any sound my footsteps may make.

"Well, you're here to help me with a little something," Sophia says as she moves forward and leans over Drake, her hands going either side of him to rest on the back of the sofa.

"Oh yeah? And what might that be?" Drake asks, practically salivating. Her position totally blocks me as I walk up behind them and tap Sophia on the bottom of her back to let her know that I am in position and ready to start the game.

"Revenge," she says before she pushes herself away from him and moves to the side. For a second, Drake looks dumbfounded, and then his eyes find mine.

"Hello, Drake," I say, a shit-eating grin on my face.

He looks from me to Sophia and then back to me. "Oh, I see, you girls want a little three-way action?" He moves his hands to his crotch and cups himself over his jeans. "I always knew that you'd see sense, Natalie."

I throw my head back and laugh. *God, he's such an asshole.* "You'd like that, huh?" I say as I fold my arms across my chest.

"Fuck yeah, and I can guarantee that you'd have a better time with me than with that old-age-pensioner you're currently fucking."

I refrain from rolling my eyes at his lower than low comment because he knows fuck all about my life. "You think you can handle two of us?"

"You know it," he says as he tries to reach forward to touch me, but I slightly step back and out of his reach.

"But what about three of us?" I say and his eyes go a little wide.

"Three?" he squeaks, like he can't believe his fucking luck. I refrain from laughing in his face... not yet... later my victory will come.

"Uh huh." I nod and step to the side to reveal the third person to join this party.

Stepping from the shadows at the back of the room is Marshall.

I keep watching Drake and think that his eyes are about to bug out of his head.

"Oh no, I ain't into men," Drake says as he shakes his head.

"Oh, Drake," I say as Marshall stops beside me, Sophia coming to stand at my other side. "You don't get to make the rules." I step towards him and bend down so that we're eye level. "And this is no fucking orgy," I say through gritted teeth as I take him by surprise and grab him by the throat, pushing him back on the sofa, my knee hovering over his scrawny dick.

"You don't want to do this, Natalie," Drake whispers because my hold on his neck is so fucking tight. I may be petite, but I know how to make someone stop breathing.

"You have no idea what I want," I snarl at him, inches from his face as I bring my knee closer to his crotch. "You see, you seem to think that you have a hold over me, that by dangling the fact that you think you know who I'm fucking is some sort of price over my head, but actually, all you've done is fuel my desire to cut your balls off."

"Wait a minute," he says as his hands rest on my arm, his grip slowly tightening as he tries to get my hand off his throat. I loosen my grip, but not because he's trying to exert some pathetic show of manliness, but because I want to and because this party is far from over.

I feel Marshall step up behind me and I smirk. "There's a clear difference this time, Drake..." I pause for a second, more for effect than anything else. I move my lips by his ear and whisper, "This time I'm prepared." And with that, I move away from him quickly, catching him off guard so he lets go of me, and I step back, allowing Marshall to step in and take my place as he pins a panic-stricken Drake to the sofa.

Drake looks to me with fear in his eyes. He knows of Marshall's rep, and he knows that shit isn't going to go smoothly for him here.

Sophia goes over with the cable ties and rope that will

keep Drake in place as I get the truth out of him and then Marshall gets to fuck with him, mess him up a little and send him out of here a shadow of the asshole that he usually is.

"What's the matter, Drake?" I say sweetly before my voice turns hard and I add, "I thought you liked to party?"

CHAPTER THIRTY-ONE

Marshall

THAT SMELL.
Fear.
I live for it.
Gets my adrenaline rushing like nothing else.
Well, nothing except for the woman that is currently stood beside me, waiting for me to mess shit up. Sophia. Damn she gets under my fucking skin and makes my dick harder than rock. And she also fucking hates me. I see the rage in her eyes when she looks at me. Turns me the fuck on, if I'm honest.

Nothing better than the push and pull of your heart and your head. I should know. It happens on the daily, but that's a story for another day, and right now, I need to take that frustration out somewhere... and tonight, it's Drake McCoy that is going up against me. Good fucking luck, buddy.

I turn my attention to Drake and note the hanging of his head, the defeat in his stooped shoulders and the tears that drip off the end of his nose. Fucking pussy. It almost upsets me when they act like this; hard done by, like they don't deserve it, as if we should take mercy on them. I prefer it when they give me a little challenge, fight back, make me work for the end result, makes the victory all the more sweeter.

Natalie turns to face me, giving me a nod, letting me know that she's done and now it's my turn. She got the confessions she needed, all recorded and backed the fuck up by the sound system in this room which links straight to my computer and makes a copy.

She obviously had a little slap and tickle with the guy, a jab here, a punch there as she was making him confess to all his dirty little secrets. He sang like a goddamn canary. All those months of taunting her, having digs at her, trying to intimidate her and he pissed himself as soon as she started interrogating him.

Natalie walks to the side and I step forward, the evil smirk on my face not lost on Drake as he looks up at me.

"Please," he whispers, the fear multiplying.

I crouch down, allowing my forearms to rest on my knees, my hands dangling in front of me. "Oh, come on now, Drake, don't disappoint me," I begin. "At least make an effort to plead your case instead of just saying please."

"What's the point?" he says, still whispering. "You're just going to do what you want anyway, it's hardly fair with me cable-tied to the fucking chair like some kind of hog roast."

Huh.

He makes a good point.

"Untie him," I say out loud. The shock on his face is priceless as Natalie goes behind him and cuts the ties off, freeing his hands and legs, allowing him a moment to think that he may just get the upper hand here. Pah, it's laughable. Fucking upper hand, yeah, right.

"There we go," I start, a smirk on my face. "Now we're even." I hold my hands out either side of me.

"Hardly," he mutters.

"What was that? Speak up so the whole room can hear you, Drake," I say before the smirk drops from my face and a hardened look takes over.

"Well, it's hardly fair seeing as I've already been hit. I mean, talk about making sure I'm not at my best..." His voice fades off as I stare him down. Stupid twat.

"You're just going to have to push through and do your best, Drake, because I'm hungry and it's been a while..."

I move forward, my fist connecting with his jaw, his head flying back, his legs stumbling as he tries to regain his footing. I let him, I wait, I exert some patience because there is nothing worse than an enemy that already thinks they have lost. There's no fun in that.

The last person I had to fuck up was lured like a snake into the viper's den, and then I was the one that had the pleasure of watching the life slowly seep out of him.

I'm not an asshole, I only punish those who deserve it, but those that need to be punished don't get let off lightly, and Drake will be no exception.

I'll leave him able to hobble out of here, but anything else is fair game.

You do not come up against me and win.

I'm the only winner.

And as me and Natalie gear up to say we want to take over the running of things from my parents, it's all good practice for when we actually do get to play with the big boys.

I can't wait until they see me in charge.

Cocky as shit Marshall.

Running the underworld.

I was born for this role.

Made to be a leader.

And with Natalie by my side, we will be the next fucking level. A force to be reckoned with.

A duo that takes no shit and is feared by everyone.

We have high standards to live up to... her parents, my parents... but we're ready.

I see the same hunger in Natalie's eyes as I do my own.

It's time. And as I let Drake get a couple of hits in, I smile knowing that this world will be all ours.

I smile because my story is about to begin... and I can't wait to see where the journey takes me...

CHAPTER THIRTY-TWO

Natalie

I CROUCH in front of Drake, his head hanging down, blood dripping from his face and from various parts of his body. Marshall certainly put on quite a show as he cut, sliced and tortured the asshole sat in front of me.

I don't feel sorry for Drake. He came for me, and this is the end result.

No one threatens me.

No one else calls the shots.

I do.

Sometimes you just have to bide your time, wait it out, look for the perfect moment to take your revenge.

Not only have I got this little bitch confessing to everything that he has done wrong, but I also have the satisfaction of knowing that he can't hurt me, he can't uncover my truths, and he will never come for me again.

"I think our work here is done," I say in a voice full of hate. "If you ever try to come after me again, I will destroy you, do you understand?" I ask Drake as his head still hangs. "I asked you a fucking question," I say as I hit his leg with my fist. He lets out a pained squeal in response.

I wait a beat to see if he will say anymore, but I don't think he can voice any words. Must be because of the Chelsea smile that Marshall gave him.

I stand up, feeling an overwhelming sense of power engulfing me.

My parents don't think I want this life, but I absolutely do, and I think I need to tell them that sooner rather than later.

"You good to sort the clean up?" I ask Marshall who is sat on the edge of his desk, surveying his handiwork with a smirk.

"Already on their way, Natty," he says, and I know that we are going to make a great fucking team.

I turn to Sophia next, who is beside Marshall. "You good?"

Her wide eyes look to me and she nods her head. I frown because I'm not convinced that she is okay, but I need to go and see Jesse right now and tell him that our worries are over.

"I'm going to head out, got a few more things to take care of," I tell them both.

"No worries, we got this." Marshall winks at me and I give him a smile. He's a crazy motherfucker, but I wouldn't want anyone else in my corner with me.

"I'll follow you out," Sophia says, her voice quiet. She pushes herself off the desk and walks over to me. Something isn't right and a part of me hopes that I haven't lost her as a friend.

I turn to the door and open it but turn back to speak to Marshall before I leave. "Hey, Marshall," I begin, and he looks at me. "Make sure you don't kill him." I nod at Drake.

"Please, Natty, I know the rules," he says with a sly smile.

I grin and walk out of his office, Sophia behind me.

Before I manage to get to the top of the stairs, she grabs my arm and I turn around.

"What's wrong, Sophia?" I ask. "Shit, it was too much, wasn't it?"

She starts to shake her head slowly from side to side, and I feel even more confused.

"Sophia," I say, placing my hands on the tops of her arms. "What is it?"

"I..." She closes her eyes for a second before opening them again and hitting me with her stare. "I just... Natalie, I really got one hell of a kick out of everything that just happened in there." She's whispering, like she is scared to voice these words.

My lips pull into a small smirk.

"It's not funny," she says, playfully swatting my arm as I drop my hands to my sides.

"It kinda is."

"What is happening to me, Nat?" she asks as she runs both of her hands through her hair.

"Well," I start, putting my arm around her shoulders. "I think this means that you're meant for this world."

I begin to move us forward and we descend the stairs as I watch her from the corner of my eye, her mouth opening and closing several times as she tries to find the right words to say.

When we get to the bottom of the stairs, I turn to her and wrap my arms around her, placing my lips by her ear and whispering, "Welcome to the family, Sophia."

CHAPTER THIRTY-THREE

Jesse

IT WAS the blow to my head that knocked me out cold.

One swift hit and I was down.

Fuck.

I groggily lift my head, my eyes squinting from the harsh, bright lighting.

I groan as my neck hurts, wanting me to drop my head back down, but I can't do that because I need to know where the fuck I am, who the fuck brought me here, and why the fuck I am tied to a chair. My arms and legs are both tied with some thick ass rope, and there is no way I am escaping from here.

Whoever wants to keep me here has done a damn good job of making sure there is no possibility of me ever breaking free from these ropes.

My ears prick at the sound of shoes clicking against the concrete floor. I freeze, straining to hear everything, hoping to use something against the asshole that has brought me here.

"Well, well... Nice of you to finally wake up and join us," says a voice that I have heard before. A voice that I know. A voice that is going to utterly destroy me if I don't tread very carefully.

As they walk beside me, I watch out of the corner of my eye. They walk until they are standing in front of me, arms folded across their chest, bad as fuck look on their face.

Shit.

Paige Valentine.

The mother of the woman I am in love with.

The woman that I hope will come to see me as a son-in-law one day, regardless of the fact that she currently has me tied to a fucking chair.

But there is nothing motherly about her right now. She means business. Dressed in black leather trousers, black high-heeled boots and a black vest top, it appears I may be about to meet my maker.

"So, *Professor*," she starts as she walks towards me and bends down so we're eye level. "Tell me, what makes you think that you can take your dick and put it in my daughter?"

Jesus.

Straight to the point.

Before I can think of any kind of response, she hits me across the face, hard. That fucking stung a little bit. I grit my teeth as I turn back to face her.

"I asked you a fucking question," she says, her jaw tense, her eyes blazing as if she is hungry for this, to bring me down, to make me pay. I guess she's missed out on teaching asshole's lessons since she gave up her throne, but I am no asshole, and I need to win this woman over.

"I love her," I say and am rewarded with another hit

across the face, this time on the other cheek, so at least the pain is even on both sides now.

"Wrong answer."

"It's the truth," I say, desperate for her to let me speak. "Please, let me explain—"

"Explain?" she says as she stands tall, crosses her arms over her chest and takes a couple of steps back. "And what is it that you would like to explain? How you took advantage of my daughter?"

"No, please, it was never like that," I plead, knowing that I need to come up with better answers, but my brain doesn't want to cooperate.

"Of course it wasn't," she says as she paces in front of me from side to side, sounding bored to death. "Let me guess... It just happened, you couldn't control yourself, you couldn't bear the thought of upsetting her, you couldn't say no..." She stops talking and stares at me, and if looks could kill, I'd be a fucking goner right now. "But no is exactly what you should have said."

"Look, I get that you're not happy about this—"

"Pah," she says loudly, cutting me off again. "Not happy? You're damn fucking right I'm not happy."

"Will you please let me talk?"

"And why the fuck should I let you do that?" she says, a dangerous edge to her voice.

I reply before my brain engages with my mouth. "Because I have a fucking right to defend myself, and because I fucking love Natalie." I speak loudly and I hold her stare. My jaw clenches, and I know that I cannot back down here. I have to prove to her that I love Natalie more than life itself. I also need to show her that I am not some weak-ass pussy even though I am tied to a goddamn chair.

"Hmm, so he has balls," she mumbles, more to herself than to me.

"I would never disrespect Natalie, I did not take advantage of Natalie, and I would never fucking hurt Natalie. I know that it looks bad, I know that I am older than her and that I am her professor, but I swear to you that I never intended for anything to happen, and actually, I *did* try to stop it..." My voice fades off as I remember that day in my office when Natalie was on my desk, her legs spread, her finger dipping in her pussy. I quickly cut the memory off because now is not the fucking time.

"So, you're saying that my daughter took advantage of you?" she questions with her eyebrow raised.

"No. I'm saying that neither of us could stop what we felt for each other," I say, unable to fully explain the way we feel. "We fit together. She means everything to me, and I know that I would die to protect her." I inject so much fucking passion into my words that there is no way she can disbelieve me.

She seems to think about what I have said as she looks around the room. "You know, I've missed this place," she says, holding her hands out either side of her as she continues to look around. "This place used to be my salvation. A place where I would bring all of those that had done me wrong. A place where I would tell home truths to those who didn't want to hear it." She looks back at me with an evil glint in her eyes. "A place where I would end the bastards that tried to take me down or hurt the ones I love."

Shit.

She has no intention of listening to me.

She doesn't care about the fact that I am madly in love with her daughter.

All she sees is a teacher fucking his student.

And as she advances on me whilst I sit helpless, I realise that no matter what I say right now, it won't make a blind bit of difference.

Paige Valentine hates me.
Paige Valentine is going to make me pay.
Paige Valentine will be the one to kill me.

CHAPTER THIRTY-FOUR

Jesse

I DON'T THINK I have ever felt fear like this before.

But it's not fear for myself, it's fear for Natalie.

My Natalie.

The woman I love fiercely and who I would do anything for.

She will not forgive her mother if she kills me.

I have to stop Paige from losing her shit with me.

I have to make Paige see that me and Natalie are the real fucking deal.

"Paige, please—"

"Don't you dare speak my fucking name," she shouts. "You don't get to act like you know who the fuck I am."

Shit.

"Okay, I'm sorry, I didn't mean to overstep the mark," I say, and I can hear the desperation in my voice and I fucking hate it. "I just... Please, don't—"

"I suggest you give up begging, because there isn't any

amount of begging that can save your ass," a deep voice says from behind me, and I know that Joey Valentine has just rocked up to this shit-show of a party.

"Hey, babe, you're just in time," Paige says with a smile on her face as she magically pulls a knuckle duster from behind her and puts it on.

Oh my fuck.

I'm screwed. Totally and utterly screwed.

"Look, I know what it looks like, but I do love your daughter, and if you go ahead and do this, just know that she will never forgive you," I say because I really have nothing left to lose at this point. They're going to kill me, and probably torture me before they decide to end my life.

"And what the hell do you know about me and my daughter?" Joey asks, his face stern, his tone deadly.

"I know more than you think, and I know that she will never get over this. I haven't fucking brain-washed her, I haven't done anything against her will, and I certainly wouldn't ever put her in a position like the one you are about to."

It takes about three seconds for the punch to land on my jaw and make me spit blood. Clearly, I pushed Joey too far, but I don't care. If I am ever to get out of this situation and be a part of Natalie's life, they have to know that I won't just take shit lying down. I have to own what I have done and give back as good as I get.

"I'm not quite sure what part of this that you're not getting, but you are in no position to lecture either of us about how we should handle anything when it comes to Natalie," Joey says.

"I'm not lecturing you; I'm just trying to make you see that she wouldn't want this," I argue.

"Because you made her think that way," he says.

"Really? Do you honestly think that I could have made

your daughter do anything that she didn't want to do? You know that you raised a fucking strong woman, so don't try and play it down," I retort.

I spit some more blood out of my mouth and hang my head. "I love her, and it's as simple as that," I say quietly. "We never planned it, I tried to resist it but she's an incredible woman who I am in awe of every single day." I realise I've gone from arguing my case to being a soppy sod in the space of a few minutes, but if there was any time to be real and dig deep, then it is now.

"I'm older, sure. I know it's not ideal, but if we had been two people that had met in a bar over a drink, then this would be a totally different ball game," I continue, my eyes fixed on the ground. "I have wished many times over the last few months that I had never become a professor, but then, if I hadn't, I may never have met Natalie, so I can't completely regret my choice to teach. I don't expect either of you to believe me or understand where I'm coming from, because I get it, you're her parents and I have crossed so many lines I'm pretty sure all you see is a shady bastard sat before you, but just know that I would cross those lines again and again because she is it for me."

I look up to deliver my final line with what I hope is enough to convince them that I am the real deal and not some pervy professor getting his kicks. "She's my ride or die."

CHAPTER THIRTY-FIVE

Natalie

You know, I really thought that tonight was going to amazing after dealing with Drake. I left Tulip on a high, energised from stopping the threat that wanted to bring me and Jesse down.

But then I got to Jesse's house and there was no answer.

I rang his phone several times, no answer.

I waited outside of his place in my car for a little while, and there was no sign of him.

His car sat in the driveway, but no lights were on in his house.

I know the guy is entitled to go out without informing me of his every move, but my gut tells me that something is off. Something doesn't add up. Something is bugging me.

I get back out of my car and retrace my steps up Jesse's path.

I peer through the ground-floor windows, but it's too dark to see anything.

Where are you, Jesse?

My phone starts to ring, and I pull it out of my pocket, seeing that it is Marshall calling me.

"Hey," I say as I answer. "Is something wrong? Did the clean-up not go to plan?"

"The clean-up is fine, all taken care of and the damaged product has been delivered back to its parents with the threat of them needing to get the hell out of dodge."

"Good. So why are you calling me?"

"Natty..." His voice fades off and I get a sinking feeling in my gut.

"What is it?"

"Jesse is with your parents."

I feel as if the ground has been moved from underneath my feet and my knees buckle. I fall to the ground, shock rendering me speechless.

"They're at your mum's old place," he continues.

"How do you know this?" I whisper.

"Drake."

"Drake?" I question.

"He dropped the bomb on me when we were leaving his parents' house. Fucking struggled to whisper it, but I heard him loud and clear. And we both know that when any of our family have someone they want to deal with, they always end up in the basement of your mum's old place."

"Fuck," I say as I gather my wits and run back to my car, jumping in and starting it before throwing my phone down on the passenger seat and screeching off in the direction of my mum's old house that the 'family' members have used for years.

"I'll meet you there, Natty."

I hear the beep of the phone, indicating that Marshall has hung up, but my only focus is on the road ahead and getting to Jesse before my parents do something that I will never forgive them for.

CHAPTER THIRTY-SIX

Natalie

THE SECONDS TICK BY, and then finally, the house comes into view. The gates are open, and I screech onto the drive, barely stopping the car before I'm climbing out and running to the front door, pushing it open. Rome is stood at the entrance but doesn't look the least bit surprised by my appearance. I guess he was watching the monitors and it alerted him to my presence.

"Where are they?" I ask him.

"Natalie, you really shouldn't be here," he tells me, but like fuck am I listening to that.

"They downstairs?" I say as I walk off in the direction of the basement.

"Natalie," I hear Rome say behind me before I feel him grab my arm. I yank it from his grasp and whirl around, pinning him with my death stare.

"Don't fucking do that," I say, plenty of warning behind my words. Rome just looks at me, and he knows not to try anything else. My parents may have Jesse, but they would also gut him like a fish if he put his hands on me again without my permission. The blood is pumping in my ears and my urge to get to Jesse grows with every passing second.

Rome nods at me and I run down the hallway, flinging the door open to the basement, quickly making my way down the steps and to the bottom. And there, tied to a chair, helpless, is Jesse. His head is hanging forwards and my parents are stood in front of him, watching him before their eyes move to me as I walk further into the room.

The tension in the room is off the fucking scale as I glare at them, my eyes moving down to see the fucking knuckle duster that my mum is wearing. "What have you done?" I say quietly before rushing over to Jesse and kneeling in front of him.

I place my hands on his knees and gently say his name. "Jesse." The desperation in my voice for him to lift his head and look at me, speak to me, show me that he is okay is overwhelming.

I furiously start to try and untie his legs before moving around him and releasing his hands from the ropes. I had to use my pocketknife because the ropes were so tight. I move back to the front of him, and his head is still hanging down.

Fuck.

"Jesse, please, wake up," I say as tears begin to slide down my cheeks. I hold his face in my hands, gently cupping his cheeks as I will him with everything that I am to open his goddamn eyes. I look at his face and see the cut to his cheek, the bruise that is forming on his jaw and the one that blemishes his beautiful skin by his eye.

I place his forehead against mine and close my eyes. "Jesse, I love you, please open your eyes," I whisper as I try to stop the tears that are still escaping from my eyes. I know that he's still breathing, so I know he isn't dead, but fuck knows what my parents have done to him that I don't know about.

My parents.

The two people who are supposed to love and protect me have hurt me in a way I never thought possible.

"If he doesn't forgive all of this, then I'm done with you," I grit out loudly, so my parents know that I am talking to them.

"Natalie, baby—"

"No, Mother," I say as I gently move away from Jesse and turn around, standing up and facing them both. Fury moves through me like nothing I have ever experienced before. "You had no fucking right to do this."

"We had every right to do this," my dad chimes in.

"Why? Because you're a Valentine? Because you once ran the underworld? Please, Dad, don't be so fucking cliché," I say, and I can see that they are both shocked by the way that I am speaking to them, but I don't fucking care. "You are my parents, but I will never forgive this if he leaves me, I will never forget that you made him give me up."

My chest is heaving, my breathing erratic.

"Natalie, he's your professor," my mum says, and I can see the pain on her face, but I can't find it in me to feel anything other than disgust right now.

"So? Do you think that I don't know my own mind?"

"Honey, please, calm down," my mum says, and I look at her in disbelief.

"Calm down? Are you joking right now?" I seethe. "Answer me this, if this had been Dad tied to a chair, would you have remained calm?"

My question stumps her because I absolutely know that she would have lost her shit by now. Her silence speaks volumes.

"That's what I thought," I say. "Out of everyone, I

thought that you two would understand." I am so fucking disappointed in them right now.

"We're trying to understand, Natalie, but Jesus Christ, you have to realise that this is a hell of a lot to digest," my dad says, and I see the despair in his eyes. "Why didn't you just tell us?"

I scoff. "Oh please, like I could have done that." I roll my eyes. "You would have flipped your shit just like you have done right now."

"You don't know that because you didn't give us the chance to understand, you gave us no explanation and then we had to find out from Drake McCoy that your secret boyfriend was your professor... I'm sorry, baby girl, but that is not how we do things, and you know it," my dad says as he takes a step towards me. "We have always been open and honest with each other, so when you keep important shit like this quiet, you have to realise that there will be consequences and the choices that me and your mum make are only those that we believe to be in your best interest."

I sigh and close my eyes.

He's right.

I've never kept anything from them before.

Until Jesse.

Fuck.

I've messed this up so badly.

"I didn't want you to freak out and go all crazy," I admit as I open my eyes and blink away the tears that are trying to fall once again.

"I'm not going to stand here and lie to you, Natalie, so I will admit that yes, we would have freaked out, but what parent wouldn't? But we also would have listened to you. We love you and only want you to be happy, and if Jesse makes you happy then we would have accepted that... eventually," he adds with a small smile.

I bite my bottom lip to stop it from trembling.

"You should never ever be worried about coming to us, Natalie. We are always here for you, and if Jesse really loves you then there is nothing that will ever keep him from you," my dad says as he steps forward again and puts his arms around me, pulling me in for a hug. I cry against his chest because he's right with everything he said, and it fucking kills me that I wasn't just truthful in the first place. I should have had more faith in them, and I shouldn't have been such a chicken shit.

"Ugh, you're right," I say as I push away from him and wipe the tears from my face. "I'm sorry I didn't tell you; I've fucked everything up."

"No, baby," my mum says as she moves around my dad and puts her hands on my shoulders. "I'm sorry that you felt you couldn't tell us, and for that, I will always have regret. We are the two people who you should be able to trust above all others, but I do understand why you didn't tell us... I mean, we do fly off the handle occasionally."

I raise one eyebrow at her. "Occasionally?"

"Don't push it," she says with a smile.

"What if he doesn't want to be with me after this, Mum?" I whisper.

"He will," I hear said from behind me and I whirl around, Mum's hands dropping from my shoulders.

"Jesse," I say as I go over and kneel in front of him. "Are you okay?" *Stupid fucking question, Natalie, of course he's not okay.* "Ignore that question, I'm just so glad you're awake." He takes my hands in his and leans his forehead against mine.

"I love you," he says and fuck if my heart doesn't melt right there. "There is nothing that would stop me wanting to be with you, Natalie. Always."

"Always," I say as I smile at him.

CHAPTER THIRTY-SEVEN

Jesse

I DON'T KNOW what the fuck happened, but I've opened my eyes to see Natalie kneeling before me.

A vision in the madness of this moment.

I don't hesitate to tell her I love her because I still don't know if I am going to get out of here alive. I'd like to think my chances are better because Natalie is here, but I am in a room with Paige and Joey Valentine so anything could still happen.

"I'm so sorry, Jesse," Natalie whispers, but this isn't her fault. I don't want to put blame on anyone.

We were just two people who fell in love.

Her parents are just doing what they think is right to protect her because they love her too.

I hold no malice. I hold no grudge. It is what it is and now we have to try and make the best of it, if they will let me.

"You shouldn't be the one apologising, Natalie," Joey says, and I move my head away from Natalie's to see him stood behind her, hands in his pockets. "It should be us saying sorry."

Well, fuck. I wasn't expecting that. My eyes go wide as Paige steps up beside Joey. To be honest, out of the two of them, she probably worries me the most... maybe it's because she threw the punches and put on the fucking knuckle duster... either way, she is going to be a tough nut to crack. She may be older now, but damn can she pack a punch.

"I apologise for that," Paige says as she points to my face. "And that, and that," she finishes as she points to the other two marks on my face. I see Joey take Paige's hand, and I know that this must be hard for them and it's now my job to make them see that I am the man that they think I am.

"It's okay," I say with a casual flick of my hand. "I know that things aren't going to be easy to start with, but I love your daughter and I'm going to prove that I am all in and not just living out some goddamn fantasy."

Paige just nods her head at me but says nothing.

"You know that if you ever hurt her, you're dead, don't you?" Joey says and I answer him without hesitation.

"Yes."

"Good. Wouldn't want you to think that we'd let you walk away with the use of your legs or anything like that," Joey says, his jaw set, his eyes hard and a sly smile on his face.

"Dad," Natalie says, her voice holding a hint of warning.

"Nope, I'm allowed this as your father, I'm allowed to threaten to bust his kneecaps and make sure he dies a slow death, it's my right," Joey says with a grin which makes Natalie laugh. Guess I better get used to this kind of humour.

"We're going to go upstairs, so whenever you two are ready to come up, we will be waiting," Joey says, his voice a little softer. Joey takes Paige's hand and leads her out of whatever this room is. A basement? A torture chamber? Whatever it is, I'm glad that it looks like I will be walking out of here, kneecaps intact.

Natalie waits for them to disappear before she speaks. "If you only said those things to ensure that my parents didn't end you here and now, then I understand. I also understand if this is all too much for you. My family are a lot to handle—"

I place my finger over her lips to stop her from talking.

"Natalie, I meant every word of what I said. There is nothing and no one that will stop me ever wanting to be with you," I tell her, looking deep into her silver pools.

"You mean that?" she whispers against my finger and I drop my hand from her face.

"Never meant anything more." I smile at her and I see relief wash over her. "Always, baby."

"Always," she says before I place my lips on hers, kissing her softly, gently.

"Guess I better get used to living life in the fast lane, huh?"

Natalie chuckles before that twinkle that I love returns to her eyes. "Welcome to the dark side."

CHAPTER THIRTY-EIGHT

Natalie

JESSE and I make our way back upstairs and away from the basement. I don't know how he can be so forgiving in such a short space of time, but Jesse is one of a kind, and he's all mine.

We reach the top of the stairs and I lead him down the hallway until we get to my mother's old office, where my mum and dad are sat side by side at a table to the right. They both look at us as we enter the room, and I have to remind myself that everything is going to be okay.

"Come and sit down, we need to talk about a few things," my dad says, gesturing to the unoccupied chairs on the opposite side of the table. We both take a seat and I look at my parents, waiting to see what they are going to say, but then I decide to trump them with my news first.

"Drake has been dealt with," I inform them, and I watch as their faces remain stoic except for the slight raise of my dad's eyebrows. You would miss the action if you didn't know them very well.

"Dealt with?" he asks me, and I can't help the slight smirk that graces my lips.

"He won't be bothering any of us again," I say with a nod of my head.

"Huh," my dad says. "Care to fill us in?"

"I just gave him a little taste of what would happen if he continued to threaten me," I say with a shrug.

"He threatened you?" my dad says, leaning forwards in his seat.

"Yes. And it was Drake that attacked me outside Tulip."

"Why didn't you say anything?" my mum asks, her face still giving nothing away.

"Because I was handling it," I grit out. "He knew about me and Jesse, he held it against me, so I took matters into my own hands and taught him a lesson... One that he won't be forgetting in a hurry."

My dad seems to relax a little as he leans back, his elbows resting on the arms of the chair and his fingers going underneath his chin, acting as a steeple. "I see."

"The thing is, Dad... I want to be a part of this life," I begin, holding my hands out either side of me. "I want to follow in yours and mum's footsteps, I want to run the underworld, and I know that I would do a good job." I lay it out because my last secret almost got the love of my life killed.

"But what about Uni?" my mum asks.

"I can still finish Uni, Mum. I'm only doing the law degree so that I can protect our family better and learning the ins and outs of the justice system and knowing how to fight it is going to do that."

"And what about you, Jesse?" my mum says, turning her attention to him. "What are your thoughts on Natalie wanting to take over the underworld?"

I hold my breath as I wait to see what his answer is, and I pray that this won't scare him off after everything else that has happened.

He looks at me and then reaches across, taking my hand in his and squeezing gently.

"Natalie is my life, and I will be there with her, whatever she decides, whatever she wants to do," he says, and my heart swells.

"You say that now, but you don't really know what this world entails," my mum continues.

"I have a rough idea."

My mum sits forward, narrowing her eyes on Jesse. I get the feeling she's going to be tougher to crack than my dad when it comes to her accepting me and Jesse being together.

"You're prepared to take another life? You are ready to have all of our backs, because that's what our family does for one another, and kiss goodbye to your morals? You're certain that you want to leave behind all that you know?" she questions.

"Yes," Jesse replies without hesitation. "My life began after I met Natalie. Before that, I was merely existing."

"You say that now, but once you commit, there is no backing out," Mum says, putting a little bit more pressure on. She's testing him, seeing how far she can push him, seeing if he scares easy. I think it's safe to say that he doesn't scare easy... not after everything he has been through tonight.

"I have no intention of ever backing out," he replies, holding my hand a little tighter, and I smile.

A few seconds tick by, my mum sits back in her seat, her and my dad remaining quiet as they look at one another, silent words passing between them before they look back at us.

My dad winks at me and then speaks to Jesse. "Nothing means more to us than family, and family doesn't always mean blood-related. We look out for our own, we fight to the death, and we always stick together," he begins. "Accepting you two is going to take some time, but if Natalie loves you, then we will stand by her. You ever hurt her, and we make your life a living hell. You ever fuck us over and we will torture you until you are begging for mercy. You ever think of turning your back on us, we will put a bullet in your head faster than you can blink.

"So, Jesse, you still want to be a part of our world, a part of our family?" he asks.

"Always," Jesse replies, and I smile.

This is for keeps.

We are forever.

I'm his and he is mine.

A forbidden romance.

Two souls that couldn't be kept apart.

And now a lifetime of loving one another.

We wore our poker face's, and now... Now we don't have to hide anymore.

Natalie and Jesse.

Jesse and Natalie.

You can't control who you fall in love with.

You can't stop your heart from letting someone in when it knows they are your soulmate.

"Welcome aboard, Jesse," my mum says as her smile turns into a smirk. "This is going to be fun."

CHAPTER THIRTY-NINE

Jesse
One month later

A MONTH AGO, Paige told me that this was going to be fun, but fucking hell, I didn't realise she meant that she was going to run my ass ragged and ensure that I was up to being a part of their family.

I've done shit that I never dreamed I would ever do in such a short space of time. I've been tested, and fucking hell, I've paid my dues.

I've quickly learnt that you pay dearly if you try and fuck over the Valentine's. Joey and Paige may have handed over the reins to this world a long time ago, but there is no mistake that their name still means something.

I've taunted others, I've collected money owed, I've had a couple of guys against a wall with my hand around their throat. I've threatened, I've thrown a few punches, and I have totally left my quiet life behind.

They weren't kidding when they said that my life would totally change, and I wouldn't have it any other way.

I left my teaching job because, let's face it, I severely crossed lines and felt as dead as a fucking dodo in a classroom. I may have been tested, but it's the most alive I've felt in years. Sounds crazy, but fuck, the underworld is exciting, thrilling, dangerous, and mine and Natalie's for the taking.

She's preparing to step into Meghan and Miles' shoes once she finishes her studies. Marshall will also be considered for a higher position within the family, but damn, he really is a crazy motherfucker. I've seen him in action once, and he didn't hold back as he peeled the skin off a guy that tried to fuck him over, brought the police to his door and tried to make them think that Marshall wasn't paying his taxes. Stupid, stupid man. He paid the price and I played witness. I helped clean up after and then went home, showered and washed the sins off of me, and then I fucked Natalie senseless because the adrenaline buzz I get from this life is like nothing else.

After another full-on day of learning the ropes, I walk back through the front door of my house and drop my jacket on the floor, along with my house keys and I kick off my shoes. I'm exhausted, but when Natalie appears in my kitchen doorway—in nothing but a lacy thong and matching bra—I perk the fuck up. She looks delicious, and I can't wait to taste her.

"Hey, baby," she purrs, and I march down the hallway, not stopping until I get to her and roughly take her in my arms, slamming her against the kitchen door and devouring her lips with mine. My fingers dig in as I grab her hips and lift her up, wrapping her legs around me and placing my finger at her opening as I slide the thong to one side. I plunge my finger inside of her and she gasps as I move from her mouth and bite her neck, kissing, licking, needing so much fucking more.

Our sex life has always been incredible, but when we go animal, we fucking go animal.

Her nails dig into my shoulders, and I welcome the sting.

Her fingers move to my hair, and I welcome the burn as she pulls my locks.

Her lips find mine again, and I remove my fingers from her, unbuttoning my trousers and thrusting my hard-as-rock cock straight into her. I pound in and out of her, harder, faster, bringing us both to orgasm quickly.

She screams, I growl.

Trembling in my arms from the force of her orgasm, I hold her close, unrelenting until both of us are spent and lying on the hallway floor.

Our pants echo around us as we both struggle to regain our breath.

"Mmm," Natalie moans as she drags her body on top of mine, straddling me, leaning down and placing a light kiss on my lips. "Good day at the office?"

"It wasn't too bad," I reply as I move my hands to the bottom of her back before sliding them down so they're cupping her ass cheeks.

"Well, I have to say, this kind of work suits you, Mr Marks," she purrs as she bites my bottom lip.

I make quick work of flipping our positions, so I am on top of her, caging her in, feeling her beneath me.

"I guess it does, and you know what else suits me?" I say, keeping my eyes trained on hers.

"What's that?"

"You." I connect my lips with hers and the sparks fly, like they always do, except this time, I will make love to her. This time I will take my time and feast on the woman before me. This time there will be nothing animal about it. It will just be us, a man and a woman who fell in love, showing each other just how passionate we are.

We broke the rules.

We played a dangerous game.

And we won.

They say that love conquers all, and in this case, it absolutely fucking did.

THE END

CHECKMATE

written by Lindsey Powell

PROLOGUE

Joey

Be cruel to be kind. Shit, that's been my life motto for as long as I can remember. Becoming a ruthless bastard in order to protect anyone that meant a goddamn thing to me.

I've survived in this world despite all of the odds being against me.

My name is well-fucking-known in the underworld. It's a blessing and a curse. Not many people bother me, because they know what I am capable of. They know that I follow through with my threats.

But when she walked into my life, she blew everything I ever knew to shit.

Paige fucking Daniels, the woman that invaded my cold-blooded heart and then ripped my fucking soul to shreds.

She is my kryptonite.

She is my only fucking weakness, so she had to go.

I couldn't fully bring her into my world. The guns, the violence, the drugs. To bring her in would have made her a target, and it would have shown everyone my Achilles heel.

She made me laugh.

She made me love.

And she made me break her fucking heart.

I ALWAYS KNEW that this world was cruel, but I never realised just what it would cost me in the long run.

Paige.

The woman that sets my soul on fire. The woman that has my heart. And the woman that I have to let go.

Being a leader comes with responsibility and learning to live without the things that we cherish the most.

After my meeting with Raymond, my right-hand man, I realised that I can't rule this world and keep her too. The two things don't go together. I've seen men break from losing their loved ones. I've witnessed it time and time again, and my meeting with Raymond showed me just how much he is haunted by losing his wife, Antonia. She was killed in cold-blood by another family. They wanted to hit Raymond where it hurt, and they fucking succeeded. All I can say is, they better be good at hiding, because we're going to hunt the bastards down and wipe their existence off the face of the earth.

I can't risk the same thing happening to Paige. It would kill me, eat me up and fucking destroy me if she were to be killed because of who I am.

I won't take that risk.

I have to do the right thing.

My father's words come back to haunt me. "If you love someone in this life, son, learn to let them go."

Learn to let them go.

Shit.

Hardest fucking thing I will ever have to do.

With a heavy heart, I call out her name and hear her shout, "In here, big guy."

I walk towards the bedroom, and when she comes into view, I almost lose my resolve to get her away from me. She's on the bed, naked, waiting for me, and I'm about to become the biggest asshole that she has ever met.

I HAD to push her away in the cruellest way possible. She will never forgive me, but I can live with that as long as she is safe.

Safe from my world, safe from the danger, and safe from me.

My reputation stopped me from having her.

My role in this life stopped me from having her.

Throwing her away like a piece of trash turned me into an even meaner motherfucker than I already was.

Giving up the one good thing in my life left me with a bitter taste for revenge.

I want out, and it won't be easy. She doesn't need to witness any part of what is to come. She doesn't deserve to be tainted by me any more than she already has been.

I have a plan to get the fuck out, even if I die trying.

Paige

YOU KNOW THOSE MOMENTS, the ones that hit you right at your core, and leave you feeling like you are on cloud nine?

The moments that define our lives, and mould us into who we are today.

The moments that leave us breathless, and constantly searching for the next high.

That's how he made me feel.

That's what every second of being with him felt like.

Glorious, mind blowing, all consuming.

Moments that would stay locked in my heart forever, until the day that he ripped those moments apart and shattered my heart.

LYING IN BED, naked, waiting for him to come back has got to be one of my favourite ways to kill some time. The way he makes love to me, fucks me and leaves me feeling like a goddamn goddess is like nothing else.

I love him, and he loves me.

He may act like a hard-ass, but I get to see the softer side of him, and I love every single second of it.

I don't need anything else in life other than him.

"Paige," I hear him call out. Speak of the delicious devil and he shall appear.

"In here, big guy," I shout back, waiting for him to appear and fill the doorway with his tall frame, broad shoulders, muscular arms and thick thighs, which he does no more than five seconds later.

God, he really does take my breath away.

His eyes take in the sheet that pools around me, my breasts uncovered, my nipples stood to attention. His gaze slowly moves up, his face giving nothing away, but his words make my heart start to pound, and not in a good way.

"Get dressed," he barks as he bends down and picks my dressing robe up off the floor, throwing it towards me.

"Why? Are we going somewhere?" I ask him.

"I'm not, but you are."

What?

"Excuse me?" I say as move from the bed and put the robe on, wrapping it around my body tightly.

"You need to leave, Paige," he says, causing my whole world to shift.

"Leave? Why?" I ask, wondering what happened in the last hour for him to tell me that I need to go.

"Because I said so."

"Because you said so?" I repeat his words sarcastically. "And you think that I am leaving here without a reason for this sudden turn-around?"

Jesus, yesterday he told me I was his fucking everything, and now he's saying I need to leave?

"Yes, Paige, because I fucking said so." His voice echoes around the room, his words turning my world upside down.

"But, why? What did I do?" I sound pathetic even to my own ears, but this man is my life. I can't be without him.

"You didn't do anything."

"Then what the fuck happened? You left me here an hour ago and everything was fine, but now... Now you're making me feel like I'm an inconvenience."

"Maybe you are," he says and the first piece of my heart breaks.

"You don't mean that," I whisper, shaking my head from side to side.

He scoffs. "Don't I? And what makes you the fucking expert on what I mean and what I don't?"

I take a deep breath, trying to calm the rage boiling inside of me.

"Because I know you. You don't want me to leave, so what's really going on here?" I ask, hands on hips, trying to hold my own.

"You have been nothing but a distraction when I've needed it," he says, his face hard.

"A distraction? That's bullshit," I say, struggling to understand why he is being like this.

"It's not bullshit, Paige, and we're done."

He goes to turn away from me and I panic. I surge forwards, moving around him so I am standing in front of him, stopping him from walking away from me.

"Don't do this, don't ruin us and what we have," I say as I rest my hands on his chest. He looks down, his eyes trained on my fingers as I grasp his shirt. "You love me, I know that you love me... Please don't shut me out," I plead, practically begging him not to cast me aside.

He takes a breath, I hold mine.

His ice blues connect with my stormy greys. Except, they probably don't look stormy right now, more like sad and desperately hoping that he isn't going to follow through with this.

His lips part, his shoulders tense, and I can already see that he's closing down, putting his walls into place.

"We've had fun, we've messed around, but I no longer have a place for you in my life." His words cut deep, like a knife straight to my heart.

"No," I whisper as the first tear falls down my cheek.

"Yes. I don't need a distraction anymore, Paige. You were a good fuck, but that's all it ever was for me, a fuck and nothing more."

"You're lying," I manage to say as the tears fall faster.

He shrugs his shoulders. "Believe what you want but make no mistake that we are done here."

I grasp his shirt harder, not wanting to let go. If I let go, I know that I won't get him back, and I won't survive losing him. I'll never get over the heartbreak.

"Please... Please don't do this," I say as I sob. "I love you, I love you so much."

"Well, you're going to have to learn to live without loving me. Take it and give it to someone who deserves it. I'm not the person for *you, Paige, and the longer you drag this out, the harder it will be," he says, his voice stern, never wavering.*

"Harder for who?"

His jaw tenses and he steps back until I'm no longer fisting my fingers in his shirt. My arms fall to my sides, and I know that I have lost him. The love of my life. The only man to ever make me feel.

"You need to get dressed, pack your stuff up and go, now," *he barks, ignoring my previous question.*

"You're going to regret doing this."

"I don't regret anything," *he says, and the piece of my heart that broke first has the rest of the pieces scattered around it.*

"Tell me that you don't love me, and that you never have, and I'll go," *I say, forcing him to voice the words that may shatter me beyond repair. If he never loved me, then I need to hear it.*

He takes a step forward and bends down a little, so that we are eye-level.

"I don't love you, and I never did."

The air whooshes out of me.

My legs struggle to keep me upright.

And I realise that whatever the game was here, I just fucking lost.

LOVE IS FRAGILE, like glass. If you don't handle it with care, it will fall and break, leaving tiny little fragments in its wake that you will be finding days later.

In my case, the days turned into weeks, and the weeks turned into months.

There is no end in sight for my pain.

There is no happy ending for me.

It's over.

Prince Charming doesn't exist.

True love doesn't exist.

I am living proof. Broken beyond repair and struggling to move past all that I knew.

Joey Valentine did that to me.

He crushed my soul. Trampled on it and made sure that it was ripped apart.

You see, the problem with love is that it makes you blind.

Blind to faults.

Blind to the truth, and blind to the person that you love the most in the world hurting you, like you were nothing but a fucking pawn in the game.

I was his pawn.

He played me and won.

And he's still living the high life whilst I'm roaming in the gutter.

I was just a game to him, someone to relieve him of his stress as he worked his way up to where he is today, and then he threw me away like trash.

He may have played and won, but he isn't expecting my revenge.

He won't see it coming, and I'll be the one to call checkmate.

Checkmate
Available now

ABOUT THE AUTHOR

Lindsey lives in South West, England, with her partner and two children. She works within a family run business, and she began her writing career in 2013. She finds the time to write in-between working and raising a family.

Lindsey's love of reading inspired her to create her own book series. Her favourite book genre is romance, but her interests span over several genre's including mystery, suspense and crime.

To keep up to date with book news, you can find Lindsey on social media and you can also check out Lindsey's website where you can find all of her books:

https://lindseypowellauthor.wordpress.com

- facebook.com/lindseypowellperfect
- twitter.com/Lindsey_perfect
- instagram.com/lindseypowellperfect
- bookbub.com/authors/lindsey-powell
- goodreads.com/lpow21

ACKNOWLEDGMENTS

Thank you so much for reading Poker Face! I absolutely adore writing in this world, and I'm not quite done with these characters yet.

I would love if you could leave me a review on amazon, bookbub or goodreads, they are so incredibly important, and I am thankful for each and every one.

I couldn't keep doing this without my amazing readers. You keep me writing, and I can't wait to bring you even more steamy books!

If you haven't met Natalie's parents in their own book, keep reading for a sneak peek of Checkmate, the book where it all began...

Until next time,
    Much love,
    Lindsey.

Printed in Great Britain
by Amazon